What Others Are Saying About

Failure is Not Final
Pastor Sam Rachal, Jr.

To my father in the faith, Pastor Sam Rachal, Jr., thank you for demonstrating to us "that all things are possible if we believe." As you have been a blessing to many, I am sure that others who read this memoir will be blessed, inspired, and motivated to "press for the high calling." May God continue to bless you and yours . . . exceedingly, abundantly . . . Love always.

—*Deacon William Jones*

I found this inside look into the life of a pastor and his church to be eye-opening in surprising ways. Pastor Rachal honestly illustrates that we are all human and "but for the grace of God go I." If a pastor can fail and still do the Lord's work, then we know we are all capable of doing great things through Christ who strengthens us.

—*Tyler R. Tichelaar, PhD, author of*
the award-winning Narrow Lives

Pastor Rachal's story provides a valuable example of the many ways God can work in the lives of human beings. The beginning shows us how God continued to seek one man out to bring into His flock, even when he resisted. Then Pastor gives us an honest, insightful, and engaging account of his own struggle to stay true to the Word while shepherding others, even in the face of temptation. Finally, this book is a lesson to us all about the power of forgiveness and redemption. It reminds us not only to stay faithful to God, but of God's faithfulness to us as well.

—*Elizabeth Blandin, teacher*

After twenty-four years of knowing Pastor Sam Rachal, Jr., I still have the same respect and admiration I had for him in 1988. He is a man of God who has shown his humanism by exhibiting humbleness, vulnerability, strength, and a willingness to learn from others and always be led by God. To me, Pastor is a teacher, leader, counselor, and mentor. Still twenty-four years later, I hear his messages of "Let go and let God," "If you pray, don't worry, and if you are going to worry, don't pray," and "When two or more are gathered in His name, God is in their midst." It was only God that led our paths to cross. Thank you, Jesus! Amen!

—*Jacquie Curry, member of*
Mount Zion Missionary Baptist Church

But God had a plan. He took a bad situation and used it for good. For he used Sam Rachal, Jr. to rebuild a turbulent-damaged vessel and fertilize the spiritual growth of Mt. Zion Missionary Baptist Church. Under Pastor's leadership, he taught us to keep our eyes on God, trust Him, and know that He will supply all of our needs. He wielded the skills and talents of the faithful members and instituted Christian education programs, training activities, and taught us how to use our God-given gifts. Through Pastor's leadership skills and his faith in God, he moved Mt. Zion to a new spiritual level. He demonstrated his understanding that one must commit to developing self before he can motivate development in others. Thank you, Pastor Rachal, for teaching me (us) that nothing is more powerful than God's Word, love, and protection.

—*Linda Yerger, member of*
Mount Zion Missionary Baptist Church

Pastor Sam Rachal, Jr. came into our lives as the pastor of Mount Zion Missionary Baptist Church. He has been and still is a mentor, a counselor, a teacher, a brother in Christ, and as close as a real brother, offering kind words of advice and comfort. We shall always be grateful for the Christian example Pastor provides to this day.

—*Deacon Michael and Marilyn Gordon,*
members of Mount Zion Missionary Baptist Church

Failure is Not Final

The Journey from Tragedy to Triumph Requires Bold Faith

To my sister in the Lord —
"Cheryl Ann Smith"
God is always faithful even when we, His people, are non-faithful

Pastor Sam Rachal, Jr.

Pastor Emeritus Sam Rachal, Jr.

Failure is Not Final

The Journey from Tragedy to Triumph Requires Bold Faith

Copyright © 2013 by Pastor Sam Rachal, Jr.

Library of Congress Control Number: 2013910346
ISBN: Hardcover 978-1-4836-5118-7
Softcover 978-1-4836-5117-0
Ebook 978-1-4836-5119-4

All rights reserved. No part of this book may be reproduced or transmitted in any form or by any means, electronic or mechanical, including photocopying, recording, or by any information storage and retrieval system, without permission in writing from the copyright owner.

www.failureisnotfinalbook.com

Disclaimer: While the incidents and situations related in this book actually happened, some names have been changed to protect the privacy of individuals.

This book was printed in the United States of America.

Rev. date: 07/23/2013

To order additional copies of this book, contact:
Xlibris LLC
1-888-795-4274
www.Xlibris.com
Orders@Xlibris.com

Acknowledgment

The book *Failure is Not Final* had its origin as the result of a gift, a writer's journal, from a member of the Mount Zion Missionary Baptist Church of Bremerton, Washington. This member handed me a dark-red tablet and said, "Pastor, you should write a book." The comment activated some thought about writing, so I began to maintain a journal, not a daily activity, but just thoughts about myself, my duties as a pastor, and providing leadership to the flock. I must give credit to the U.S. Army for helping me to discover the qualities and skills needed to be an effective leader.

Maintaining a journal was not easy because my writing skills were below average; spelling was not my strongest asset. I give thanks to my wonderful wife, Cherry Ann "Bear" Rachal, a high school English teacher, who labored long and hard, helping me to develop my writing skills. After many business letters, recommendations, college seminary papers, and producing leadership manuals to impact spiritual growth in the church leaders, my writing skills advanced, yet there was still room for improvement.

Ms. Elizabeth Blandin, also a high school English teacher, was instrumental in giving me some additional guidance to improve my writing. Ms. Blandin and I spent many hours reading my initial outline of the book. She would always say very directly, "Why did you change from first person to third person?" "'Us' is the wrong pronoun," and "You must do a better job of describing people and places."

My wife, Cherry, and Ms. Blandin were my schoolmasters, but it was the church family of Mount Zion Missionary Baptist Church who gave meaning, impetus, and purpose to *Failure is Not Final.* Every member (including my favorite member) who worshipped at Mount Zion from 1984 to 2005 played a significant role in this book. God and His Holy Spirit, which lives in me and in the loving people He placed in my life, molded and shaped me into the pastor and leader I am today.

My wife, Cherry; our daughters, Stacie Bledsoe, Tiffany Kirkland, Amber Rachal-Carter; Jarutha Rena Rachal, my deceased daughter; and my sons, André Lamar and Sam III, are the cornerstones of my success as a husband, father, and pastor. Jarutha was a daddy's girl. During her life, she was my cheerleader. She always encouraged me to reach for the sky as long as she could share the glory.

During our time here on earth, we can expect to fail and make mistakes. We can never meet every person's expectation. What we must internalize, as Elizabeth Blandin says, is "failure is a process, not the product."

Believe it or not, failure is an integral part of human growth and development. When we fail, our task is to gain wisdom from the failure and begin at that point where we failed and move forward with tenacity. For example, the first sentence in a paragraph may be excellent, yet within the paragraph, we may find a sentence(s) that is not so grammatically correct. That is where we began anew. Accepting failure is not easy, but it can be beneficial when we learn from our mistakes.

My ambition for *Failure is Not Final* is that it shall ignite a spark in the life of an individual who has failed and just given up. Certainly, from a spiritual perspective, I hope that people whose lives have been tainted by a negative religious experience and who have given up on spiritual values will read this book and learn that all people have a soul—that inner person, that conscious part known only by you and your Creator.

Chauncey R. Piety's famous poem "I Am Living Now to Live Again" closes with this powerful statement:

> *I am living now to live again—*
> *Flesh and bone will turn to dust,*
> *But my soul, a part of the eternal God,*
> *Can live, will live, it must.*

Pastor Sam Rachal, Jr., Emeritus

Contents

Introduction	11
Chapter One: A Leap of Faith	13
Chapter Two: The Honeymoon	33
Chapter Three: The Tragedy	45
Chapter Four: The Road Back from Failure	63
Chapter Five: Failure is Not Final	75
Reflections on Our Time at Mount Zion by Edwin and Margaret Tegenfeldt	103
Papa's El Camino	109

Introduction

I preached my final sermon as pastor of the Mount Zion Missionary Baptist Church in Bremerton, Washington, in December 2005. At that time, I had served as the pastor of Mount Zion for over twenty-one years.

When I accepted the divine calling of God into the ministry, I had limited knowledge of the enormous impact this leap of faith would have on my life. My initial thoughts about the ministry focused on evangelism; I believed my expertise would lie in serving God as an evangelist traveling around Pierce, Kitsap, and King Counties in Washington State and conducting revivals, by invitation, from the pastors of the North Pacific Convention.

This vision for my future never materialized. After being licensed under the leadership of Pastor Floyd D. Bullock of the Bethlehem Baptist Church of Tacoma, Washington, my pastor sent me to Mount Zion to be the guest speaker for an Ushers Annual Program (a formal gathering of the Washington State Ushers). This visit initiated a return preaching engagement, but little did I know this invitation would develop into a pastoral assignment and years of practical application in learning humility, the fundamental venture of spiritual service.

The backdrop of my story as a pastor begins with my birth in 1935. I was born in Shreveport, Louisiana, which is dominated by Catholicism. I was the youngest child and only male with two sisters; my family's religious history was Catholic. My mother was reared as a Catholic while my father was a Baptist proselyte.

The journey of my life and my transition to another faith was one filled with peaks and valleys, rejection and encouragement, yet the adventures are still my greatest treasure. My first venture was in the U.S. Army for three years, followed by a four-year break. When I reenlisted, I enjoyed a very rewarding twenty-six years of service. Yet to be a pastor—the shepherd of God's people—there remained much more to learn. My call and acceptance to the ministry has been the greatest vocational experience of my life.

In writing this memoir, I hope to share my own spiritual journey so others can benefit from what I have learned and be strengthened in their own journeys. Most importantly, I wish to point out the places in life where I failed and how I overcame failure. Failure is not final, but simply part of being human, and I firmly believe that in every failure, there is a thread that will lead to success. Seeds to success lie in all the activities involved in the failing. What we must do is be brave enough to reexamine the activities of our labor and find the flaw; there is the starting point to success. God has a way of turning our failures into triumphs when we put our trust in Him.

Sam Rachal, Jr.
Bremerton, Washington
June 27, 2012

Chapter 1

A Leap of Faith

When you know about God's amazing grace, you will show more of God's grace—sometimes it takes a leap of faith.
—Sam Rachal, Jr.

When an individual is called to the ministry, he has an inner urge, an enthusiasm to excel; this undeniable driving force of a higher calling, this burning passion, never subsides until the individual takes a daring leap of faith.

This call was my inner feeling, a passion to grow and develop and take a more active role in the spiritual arena. I felt an inner urge within my soul that even I could not state in concrete terms. This continuous urge became more pronounced after I joined the Baptist persuasion. I was born and reared in a family that believed the Catholic dogma. The Catholic principle is as follows: "Once a Catholic, always a Catholic, and the penalty of hell if violated." This betwixt and between dilemma haunts my human heart even after joining a Baptist church. At the time, my inner person had a personal burning passion to pursue the spiritual arena, but my outer person was afraid of public opinion and ridicule by my biological family. Making that betwixt and between decision would alter the course of my life.

My family was a close-knit group who only associated with people of the Catholic faith. My sisters and I were not afforded freedom of movement except when we did things together or as a family. My sisters and I always did everything together in my formative years. Our activities were very limited, consisting of school, church, and the movies; everything else was exclusively family affairs.

Among my neighbors, I was allowed to associate with people of the Protestant faith, but on a very limited basis. My limited interaction with other children in my neighborhood had a negative effect on me personally, which became a major factor for me during my formative years. I had limited experience with freedom of movement or with making choices about rest, play, and work and how to allow time for each of these personal behaviors. My social skills were almost nonexistent. I was very unsure of myself around females even though I had two older sisters; I tended to see them more as tattletales than as my friends.

As the youngest in the family and the only boy, I became the instrument of my father's wrath. When my father would arrive home from work, he always appeared to be angry. My mother said it was because of his supervisor, but nevertheless, I always seemed to be the recipient of his frustration. When my sisters and mother would report to him the smallest incidents regarding my behavior, such as that I had been outside playing with my friends, they would make their report in such a way as to suggest that I had done something wrong; and my father would always believe them, never allowing me to explain, and then he would relieve his frustration by focusing his wrath on punishing me. I recall one time when my father came looking for me after he arrived home; he found me working in the garden. I had hoped that he would praise me for my efforts, but no matter what I did, I never received any praise from him.

During my early childhood and preteen years, my life was a mixture of punishment and harsh words of criticism, in conjunction with constant control. I was restricted from associating with various groups because of their perceived faults, but I was never allowed to test the truth of these perceptions. For example, my mother led us to believe that people whose skin was dark were unclean, so we were not allowed to associate with "those people" (we were Creole, lighter skinned than other Blacks). Even on a more basic level, I wished to learn how to swim, but I was not allowed in a pool because "you could drown since you do not know how to swim." The idea that I could not do something followed me during my formative and into my teenage years. I continually heard, "Sonny (my nickname) cannot do this or that" (such as play baseball, football, etc.). In time, however, it became my purpose to break through these limitations.

I did learn some responsibility as a teenager, such as doing my chores around the house—cleaning my room, taking out the garbage, and mowing the lawn. I also worked some outside jobs. My first job was delivering groceries in my local neighborhood. Most of the local grocery stores were operated by Italians, and they hired me to deliver food to the local neighbors. I also delivered the *Shreveport Sun*, the local newspaper.

After graduation from high school in 1954, a few of my friends and I joined the armed forces because of the GI Bill that offered guaranteed funds for college after three years of honorable military service. We all enlisted for three years.

My initial years in the U.S. Army were a totally new way of life for an immature person fresh out of high school. I experienced my first ride on an airplane and my first time out of the state of Louisiana—except for a trip to Dallas, Texas—to play in a football game.

During that time, I also drifted away from my spiritual and moral values to live life in the fast lane. The military lifestyle has an unwritten rule: "Do your duty Monday through Friday and enjoy the weekend."

The fast-lane lifestyle, from my perspective, involved abusing alcohol, womanizing, and gambling. My philosophy became "Whatever makes Sam feel good, just do it." Plus $75 a month was the most money I had ever earned. But I was wise enough to save a few dollars each month. Some of my friends helped me learn when to play and when to work, as well as a few weekends of having to work "extra duty"—a military term for punishment given out when a person fails to be at the right place at the right time.

When my three years in the army were over, I decided not to reenlist and was granted an honorable discharge from active duty in 1957. I was placed in the army reserves but set about living as a civilian. I soon discovered that the military lifestyle was totally different from civilian life. I quickly learned the responsibilities of renting an apartment and paying for utilities, food, and necessities. The funds I received when I was discharged from the U.S. Army and the money I had saved were soon depleted. Because I planned to attend college and my two sisters now lived in Los Angeles, I moved to Southern California with the intention to use the GI Bill to further my education. I completed one semester at Los Angeles City College. Working, studying, and being involved in weekend and weekday drinking parties turned out not to be profitable for a reckless, immature individual living in Los Angeles.

Since I was unemployed most of the time I lived in California, I finally decided to return to Shreveport, where I knew a few people who would give me some type of employment. I did get a job, but I also got involved with an old female friend from school, and with her, I fathered a child—a beautiful daughter, Jarutha Rena. My daughter became my pride and joy, but being a father was a new learning experience for me, and I still had some growing up of my own to do. I knew it was my responsibility to take care of my daughter, yet there were times when I failed as a father, such as spending money for my personal use that I should have used to support my child.

For a while, the fast lane remained more attractive to me than being a father and a husband, but my daughter's birth gradually led to my attempting to bring some balance into my life. In time, I married Irma, my daughter's mother. We moved to New Mexico, and after a few years, in 1962, I reenlisted in the U.S. Army, which was another major step toward my recovery from living in the fast lane.

Because I had been out of the army for more than four years, when I reenlisted, I was required to do sixteen weeks of training. Then I was deployed to Korea for one year. When I returned in 1963, I was reassigned to Fort Carson, Colorado. My son, Sam Rachal III, was born in June 1964, which gave me some additional incentives for being more responsible and serving as a better example in my home as a husband and father.

By this time, my fast-lane lifestyle had begun to affect my family and my military career, and it had come to mean for me the abuse of alcohol, womanizing, and engaging in some unlawful enterprises so I could make some extra money to support my habits and my family. I was no longer active in my Catholic faith, but to resolve some of our problems, my wife wanted us to start attending church regularly. So in the mid-1960s, I decided to join the Baptist persuasion. I had always enjoyed the Baptist worship service, and since my spiritual life was at rock bottom, I was looking for change. The church, I felt, would offer a better way of life. I always remember the preachers' sermons seemed to center on abuse of alcohol, smoking, and womanizing. Over the years,

I have learned how prevalently these vices are practiced in organized religion. I also began to see that church attendance and worshiping God were two very distinct behaviors. Some, like me, were practicing seat time (making an appearance), while others truly came to worship God. Living the Christian life encompasses much more than sitting in church while participating in vices on the side. The true Christian Life is a loyal, daily commitment to the Word of God, the Holy Bible, and the practical application of lessons learned from biblical instruction.

To my best recollection, I was formerly baptized into the Baptist persuasion somewhere between 1963 and 1965. My baptism was my first experience with being immersed in water. This form of baptism was very different from the Catholic practice; I had been baptized in the Catholic church when I was only a couple of months old. I had also received my first Holy Communion when I was seven. Confirmation as a Catholic sacrament was, at that time, conferred on children when they reached the age of twelve. This sacrament is a person's personal acknowledgment and decision to practice the Catholic faith. Communion and confirmation could be defined as marking a person's rite of passage into the Catholic church, and they are times of celebration with family and friends. In the Baptist persuasion, a person is baptized after acknowledging his/her lost condition because of sin, professing his need for a savior, and on simple faith, accepting Jesus as the Son of God, The Incarnate Savior, and then a water baptism ceremony is performed by the church pastor, usually with friends and family in attendance.

After I became a Baptist, for some indescribable reason, I began to feel a sense of sadness, primarily loneliness whenever I was in church or even driving past one. I would feel almost like I was alone in that church, abandoned by everyone else as the night was growing dark. Perhaps that sad feeling was a sign of my loneliness and the isolation I felt as a result of my upbringing where I was taught not to value myself, and that extended to a perception of the church as equally restrictive and a symbol of punishment even though I had left the Catholic church now. But perhaps it was also a deeper longing I had already, although not yet consciously, that my duty would lie in serving God. First, however, I would have a long journey to finding my way to a strong faith in God so I would be ready to serve him.

When I reenlisted in the U.S. Army in 1964, my family and I were relocated to Fort Bliss, Texas, just outside of El Paso. We lived in a small community about five miles from the base, named Sun Valley. This relatively new housing development was populated by active duty and retired military personnel.

Most of the homes in the Sun Valley community were one-level track houses with three and four bedrooms, and some had carports. That was my first experience living in a house with an evaporated cooling system. El Paso is hot in the summer, yet the cooling system made the home comfortable. We purchased our first home in El Paso for $8,000. Our monthly payment was $65, taxes and insurances included.

With my family, I visited several churches in the local community, yet we failed to commit to any church. I was then deployed to Vietnam for one year, and during my tour, my wife and children joined an independent Baptist church. When I returned home, I also joined the church. But my commitment to change from my past lifestyle was lacking. After I received counseling from the pastor, I was rebaptized, and I rededicated my life to Christ.

From that time, I became very involved with the church and served as the bus driver to bring children to the church's Sunday School. One Wednesday night, following a Bible study, the pastor approached me and asked, "Sam, what about you serving in the Junior Church?"

The Junior Church is a worship service established by the pastor to meet the needs of children between the ages of six and twelve. The sessions are divided between spiritual instructions and playtime.

I was a bit surprised by my pastor's request. My initial response was, "Who, me?"

The pastor replied, "Yes, you. Your children are active in the Junior Church, and your participation will have a great impact on them and also influence your life." He added, "Besides, Sam, because most of the children you pick up on Sunday are in the Junior Church, you will be a perfect fit for the task."

I decided to accept the challenge. I quickly found it very exciting; it tested my spiritual life and began to spill over into my personal life. Working in the Junior Church required diligent Bible study, but I saw that as an opportunity to learn more about the Bible. I had to prepare a short Bible story during Sunday morning worship service in the Junior Church, and I also had to give a short biblical message for Sunday service. Having to be prepared to speak on Sunday morning meant no more weekend partying and late-night drinking sprees.

As the Sunday school bus driver and teacher, each Saturday, my children and I visited the homes of the children who were to be picked up on Sunday morning. The Saturday visitation program was demanding and very motivational for me to develop stronger Christian characteristics. It also challenged me to reestablish my moral and spiritual values that carried over into my home and work. My children found my new task exciting because after visiting the families, I would take them to McDonald's for a treat. I believe they went along more for the trip to McDonald's than the visitation.

That was the beginning of an inner urge, an unexplainable passion to do more in the church. This passion continued even after I completed a second tour of duty in Vietnam and Korea. But first, during my tour of duty in Korea, I reverted back to my old way of life. I was stationed at Osan Air Base, which housed both Air Force and Army personnel. However, I did make Sunday morning visits to the base chapel service, where I got to know an airman who also attended the service.

One Saturday afternoon, I was on my way to the city when this airman stopped me and began to talk with me about the Lord. He asked me and continued to ask me, "Sam, are you saved?" My response was, "Man, I drive the Sunday school bus, work in the Junior Church, and I was once an altar boy in the Catholic church."

He responded, "But, Sam, are you saved?"

During this conversation, he helped me to gain a firm understanding of God's Plan of Salvation. I came to realize that it was only by God's grace and not by works that anyone can be assured of eternal salvation.

In 1974, my family and I were reassigned to Alaska for three years. I established a Junior Church there during my tour, and the same lingering, unexplainable urge continued within me. However, I never shared my feelings with anyone because I did not have words to explain the urge to do more.

My primary reason for being silent about this urge largely had to do with my Catholic background. My joining another faith had caused constant friction within my family, and now, to add another dimension, to it was frightening for me. Both of my sisters had been very supportive of me joining the Baptist church, yet my mother was a strong believer in Catholicism and that whatever the priest said was true and not to be questioned. She subscribed to the old philosophies, "Once a Catholic, always a Catholic" and "Anyone who isn't a Catholic is in danger of hellfire and brimstone."

My family and I were next reassigned to Fort Lewis, Washington, in September 1977. There we joined an independent Baptist church in Lakewood, a suburb of Tacoma, Washington. I was baptized again because during an invitation to discipleship, I surrendered my life to the Lord for full-time service.

However, because I was African American and the independent Baptist churches were predominately populated with Caucasian people, I quickly found my upward mobility in the church was stymied. Then I met an African American who was a former chaplain. His name was Reverend Hankerson. Once when we were meeting in his office, we began to talk about the ministry. He was a very firm and direct man, so he told me, "Young man, if you truly want to serve the Lord and be used in the ministry, you had better find yourself an African American church where you can develop your skills."

This statement puzzled me. I had felt that the independent Baptist churches were friendly, but I also had sensed that people of color were not given many leadership roles. So I took Reverend Hankerson's advice and joined the Bethlehem Baptist Church in Tacoma. The pastor, Rev. Floyd D. Bullock, agreed to let me establish a Junior Church there.

I also served on the Board of Christian Education.

Pastor Bullock was a man short of stature. He had a no-nonsense demeanor and maintained regular office hours, something very different from most African American churches. He was very organized and structured, so every department of the church had guidelines for its operation. His Sunday morning sermons included both teaching the Scripture and proclamation of the Word.

One Saturday afternoon in 1981, I stopped by the church and found Pastor Bullock in his office. We began to talk about Christian service and my desire to do more.

Pastor Bullock, who always projected a serious demeanor, smiled with a peculiar stare, and said, "What do you mean you 'want to do more'?"

I replied, "I do not know what I want to do. I just want to do something."

He proceeded to ask me a few questions, and then he said, "Do you feel you have been called to the ministry—called to preach?"

I hesitated for a moment, and then I said, "I enjoy your preaching, and sometimes when I am driving alone, I mimic your sermons."

He chuckled at that statement and replied, "Maybe you should acknowledge your call to the ministry."

I hesitated to answer because I thought my answer was a bit strange. Finally, I said, "Pastor Bullock, I want to preach, but my excuse for not stepping forward is because of the stage jubilation, the voice articulation, and the groaning that is displayed by some preachers." (Pastor Bullock did get excited when he preached, but not to the extent of some ministers.)

Pastor Bullock looked at me with a smile and said, "All of that is play acting, a public performance to excite the people. I would not classify that as sincere preaching."

I left his office relieved, with a renewed surge of energy. It seemed a huge load had been lifted from my body. Sunday morning, when the initiation to discipleship was extended, I went forward and took my seat in the chairs in front of the altar.

One of the deacons asked me my purpose for coming forward by saying, "Brother Rachal, do you wish to make a statement to the church?"

With a mixture of anxiety and joy, I stated, "I believe the Lord has called me to preach the Gospel."

I can say with conviction and affirmation that since that day, my urges to do more have disappeared from my thoughts and never returned. Little did I realize then that my leap of faith would present a good deal of heartache, disappointment, criticism, and depression. Yet the joy of service would be worth enduring all my heartaches. After accepting my calling into the ministry and even to this day, my turbulent years of living in the fast lane could not compare to the rejection and heartaches I would endure after accepting my call to the ministry. In the fast lane, I had created most of the problems that had confronted me, and somehow I had muddled through them. But the trials and tribulations of my future in the ministry could only have been endured by my strong conviction to serve the Lord.

In January 1982, I was licensed to preach. The Baptist guideline for preachers is that when an individual acknowledges his divine call of God to the ministry, the church where that individual is a member issues him a certificate of license to the ministry. Because I was a member of the Bethlehem Baptist Church of Tacoma, Washington, I would be under the sponsorship or tutelage of my pastor, the Reverend Floyd D. Bullock.

When I acknowledged my calling to the ministry, Deacon Elias Jones made a motion to accept my statement: "I, Sam Rachal, Jr., sincerely believe that God has called me to be a minister of the Gospel."

Deacon Jones's motion was seconded by Deacon Clinton Hightower, and the church body accepted my statement to preach. The board of deacons, which also included Deacon McAuley and Deacon Briggs, recommended to the church that I be allowed to preach my trial sermon as directed by Reverend Bullock.

The Bethlehem Baptist Church conducted a regular Sunday evening worship service which began with a Baptist training session.

The service opened with personal testimonies from members. Their testimonies centered on how the Lord had changed their lives as well as certain conditions and relationship changes they had experienced as a result of their personal prayers and supplications. The choir rendered a hymn before the sermon, and after the sermon, either the pastor or one of the associate ministers delivered the message and extended the call to discipleship. The call to discipleship is an opportunity for any individual in the audience to request special prayer, church membership, rededication, or baptism.

I do not recall the actual month and date of delivering my first Gospel message when I stood behind the pulpit for the first time, but the date on my license is January 17, 1982. I do recall my Scripture text was from chapter four of the Gospel according to Saint John, which tells the story of Jesus's encounter with the Samaritan woman. At church, I had inherited the title "The Samaritan" because of my mixed race—Creole and Black—but the title did not last very long.

The license to preach was for one year of service to allow for a period of self-examination. This period helps the individual to reexamine the question, "Was my calling a true spiritual inner conviction prompted by the Holy Spirit and confirmed by the Word of God and then reaffirmed by members of the church body?" The integrity of the persons who choose to preach must be rooted in a sincere conviction and a genuine concern for the salvation of humanity. One of my mentors, Dr. E. S. "Stonewall" Brazill, told me, "If this is not a true calling of God, people will send you back."

The moral I gathered from this statement was the following: The Christian ministry is subject to persecution, heartaches, harsh piercing comments, and criticism by members of the church and nonmembers. The committed shepherd remains faithful with a humble spirit, but the hireling, an individual not truly committed, retaliates by dictatorship rather than Biblical leadership, which, I believe, is rooted in respect, humility, and unconditional love for the Lord and all people.

During my pastoral experiences, several young men and women did accept their call to the ministry, which caused me to have a sincere appreciation for this trial period; it affords one the time to examine truly one's personal life and the Christian ministry. The title *reverend* or *minister* does elevate the individual to a higher standard of expectation within the church body and the surrounding community. For an individual who is on an ego-trip, this new title and position can and will inflate a person's opinion of himself. It is very easy to get on an ego-trip, primarily because of other people. Once an individual is given the identity of a pastor, reverend, or minister, people forget the person is still human with feet of clay. As pastors, we are humans first and subject to failure. We face the same daily distractions of the flesh as all humans. These human distractions come in many forms, including lust of the flesh, greed, and selfishness. When we hear words of encouragement and praise from our audience, while we are always the center of attention, it is difficult not to develop an inflated ego.

Because Bethlehem had two other associate ministers during my trial period, Minister Braxton and Minister Nash, I was afforded the opportunity to preach at least once a month.

Pastor Bullock assigned me to teach the New Members Class, which met each Sunday afternoon. This six-week study explored the history of the Baptist persuasion, including the Baptist Creed and why we believe what we believe. The two fundamental ordinances observed by the Baptist churches are baptism by immersion and the observance of the Lord's Supper. The classes covered the church covenant and church constitution and bylaws. Each student was given a graduation certificate after completing the six-week study.

In June 1984, about six months after receiving my license, Pastor Bullock called me to his office. There he asked me, "Brother Rachal, how would you like to go over to Bremerton, Washington, and preach for the Mount Zion Missionary Baptist Church Ushers Annual Session?"

I do not recall my exact words, but again, my initial thought was, "Who, me?"

With some apprehension, I agreed to accept the invitation. Pastor Bullock encouraged me by saying, "I recommend you accept the invitation. It will be an excellent opportunity to develop your speaking and preaching skills and get exposure to another Christian community."

I left his office with mixed emotions. "I will have an opportunity to preach before an unfamiliar audience in another city," I told myself, and that would be a challenge, but an exciting one.

I had once previously visited Bremerton in 1980 after my retirement from active duty. I had gone there seeking employment at the Puget Sound Naval Shipyard (PSNS). On that day, I had arrived in Bremerton around 3:00 p.m., unaware that was the shift-change hour for shipyard workers. As the people walked past me, they appeared to be extremely grubby. It appeared they all wore beards and were carrying lunch pails that all looked identical. Everyone coming out of the shipyard seemed to be wearing blue jeans and a heavy multicolored plaid shirt made of wool. I do not remember seeing one person of color. At the time, I thought, "What a strange town with some very unique people. A person can only reach this place by the Narrows Bridge—'one road in, and one road out.'" At that time, I was unfamiliar with the Belfair Highway through Shelton, Washington, which is another way out of Kitsap County.

Bremerton, Washington is one of the chief cities in Kitsap County, and it sits on a peninsula surrounded by the water. The peninsula is connected to the eastern shores of Puget Sound by the Washington State Ferries, which run from Bremerton to Downtown Seattle, from Kingston to Edmonds, and from Southworth to West Seattle via Vashon Island. From Tacoma, the Narrows Bridge is the gateway into Kitsap County.

Bremerton is a small quiet city with limited excitement for teenagers except for high school football and baseball games on Friday or Saturday night. Teenagers would hang out at Taco Bell, McDonald's, and a new strip mall. Most of the houses are one floor, a few are split-level, with bedrooms upstairs and the kitchen and living room on the first floor. The city's downtown consists of one main street, Pacific Avenue, and Washington Boulevard, where you enter and exit Washington Ferry Dock between Seattle and Bremerton.

Bremerton was named after entrepreneur William Bremer. According to the town history, Bremer and his brother-in-law, Henry Hensel, purchased some undeveloped land near Point Turner at the inflated price of $200 per acre and sold 190 acres to the Navy at $50 per acre; that property is today the Puget Sound Naval Shipyard.

Historically, Bremerton was populated by Caucasians, but during the 1940s, many African American families relocated to the Great Northwest from Texas, Louisiana, Mississippi, and Georgia in search of better employment. The Pacific War was at its peak, so these people were able to secure jobs because of the heavy workload needed for shipbuilding, repair, and maintenance at Puget Sound Naval Shipyard. After World War II, some of the families remained and established homes in Bremerton.

Those families needed a place of worship, and at the time, the only African American place of worship was the Ebenezer African American

Methodist Church. So under the leadership of several Black families, in 1944, the Hilltop Baptist Church formed its first Sunday school classes. In 1945, after the church building was completed on Werner Road in West Bremerton, the congregation selected the name Mount Zion Missionary Baptist Church.

October 1984 would be my first visit to Mount Zion, and I found the parishioners to be very cordial and loving people. The Reverend Leroy T. Overby was the pastor, and the congregation was populated by middle-income families, many of whom had been members since the church's founding. I later discovered that a few of the members were from Louisiana like me. The chairman of the ushers board was Bro. Fred Crumpton, a native Louisianan. He greeted me by saying, "My name is Fred Crumpton, and whatever you need, let me know."

The congregation not only enjoyed my sermon, but my friend and associate minister from my home church, Leslie D. Braxton, told me, "Man, you're on a roll, and the people were dancing in the aisles."

At that point, my first experience of preaching outside of my home church and my friend's words of encouragement gave me some assurance of a job well done.

That same month, the church requested that I come and preach for Mount Zion during the Sunday morning worship service. Then Deacon Fally Tyson, the chairman of the board of deacons, asked me to come back the next Sunday. I ended up preaching there every Sunday from late October into November.

After one worship service in November or early December 1984, Deacon Tyson asked me whether I would be interested in becoming the pastor of Mount Zion. I discussed this opportunity with my wife, who was not very happy about the thought of living in Bremerton, but she agreed to it if I felt it was what the Lord wanted me to do.

The next Sunday, I told Deacon Tyson I would be willing to accept the position if the church would have me. To become the pastor of a Baptist church, you must be approved by a two-thirds vote by the church body. The church body voted in the affirmative to select me, Rev. Sam Rachal, Jr., as pastor of the Mount Zion Missionary Baptist Church of Bremerton, Washington. At that time, I was licensed to preach, but to become the church pastor required ordination by my home church, Bethlehem Baptist Church.

Ordination includes several steps. First, a catechizing council is established by the church pastor. The candidate is given a list of questions to study, and he must be prepared to make a formal statement about his conversion and divine call to the ministry.

This process was conducted at the Bethlehem Baptist Church through the organization of Pastor Bullock. The catechizing council included Rev. E. S. Brazill as chairman, Rev. Percy Gardner, and Rev. B. A. Taylor. After the catechizing was completed, I was dismissed to allow the council to determine my credibility to be ordained. After several minutes, which felt like an hour, I was instructed to return to the council and take a seat.

Reverend Brazill said to me, "Young man, what if the council decided you're not ready to be ordained or to pastor a church? What would you say?"

I paused for a moment to collect my thoughts and relax. To the best of my recollection, I then said, "Well, I truly believe God has called me to the ministry, and I intend to continue to preach, ordained or not."

There were some responses, but I do not recall exactly what was said. Then Rev. Brazill and the council members congratulated me for my excellent display of spiritual awareness.

I was ordained the following Sunday afternoon. The Reverend B. A. Taylor preached the installation sermon; his topic was "A Sheep among Wolves." This metaphor would soon become a reality as I assumed my duties and responsibilities as pastor of the Mount Zion Missionary Baptist Church.

I was very excited about my future, but I was inexperienced at pastoring people. I had gained leadership experience in the U.S. Army, but the rules are different in the civilian world, especially when you are working with volunteers. Now I would learn firsthand how an inflated ego can soon become deflated. As a pastor, your first few months or maybe even a year with your congregation is the honeymoon period. Then the congregation and the new pastor both come to understand that the pastor does have feet of clay, and he and the congregation can both be sheep among wolves. Pastors are frail humans, as are parishioners, and they are all subject to failure. My mixed race and my Catholic background were always subject to questions through it all, but I held fast to my personal motto: "I was called by God to work for Jesus."

Chapter 2

The Honeymoon

A church family is like the bride of the pastor; first, there's the honeymoon; then true love, plus conflict, ensues.
—Pastor Sam Rachal, Jr.

There is an old cliché within both the secular and faith communities called the honeymoon period. This initial period of time begins when a new leader is elected or appointed to a new position and continues until the new pastor is acclimated into his or her new church family. The actual length of time could be one day, one week, or months. But of course, this honeymoon period has its termination point.

The honeymoon period is a time when it appears to the pastor that the entire church membership is very supportive of the new pastor. It may appear that most of the new pastor's leadership principles are accepted. The channel of communication between the new pastor and members appears to be open and honest. Most of the suggestions about minor changes are received with admiration, and the general atmosphere or spirit of the church is "We want change." Then without warning, the parable of the "Sheep among Wolves" becomes very real. It's revealed that some members of the church want change, but not all of them. A revolting attitude from these members becomes not only evident, but aggressive with a vengeance. Suddenly, the honeymoon is over.

The disgruntled group in the church has now made itself known. Masquerading as wolves in sheep's clothing, these enemies of the church become the villains of a resistance movement; they are a hostile group demanding to make their thoughts and feelings known.

When I first experienced this situation, my initial thought was, "Where were these people during the initial business meeting? Were they not the ones who received me with open arms and warm smiles of encouragement and said, "Welcome aboard"? Yes, they were welcoming and embracing in the beginning, but now I was shocked to find their true characters revealed.

I was an inexperienced and gullible pastor, and this was my first pastorate. I was also unaware of how church politics worked. The Baptist church's policies for the election of a pastor were never discussed with me, not by the election committee, and not before or after my election. After the church members had met following Sunday morning service, I had simply been informed of my new position by the chairman of the board of deacons, Deacon Tyson, and I was welcomed by the members who told me how happy and excited they were to have me as their new pastor.

Now, out of the blue, the tide was turning. My honeymoon period was over, and it left me wondering, "Why the sudden change in attitude?" I knew, from having encountered all types of people during my military service, that humans are fickle, with different personalities, but this sudden change of attitude among my congregation was a total and unpleasant surprise. I was very familiar with the behavior of worldly people, but these were Christians.

From the beginning of my service at Mount Zion, after I preached during a Sunday morning worship service, my wife and I were always escorted to lunch. We always went to eat at a buffet-style restaurant called the Royal Fork. One particular Sunday, however, we were instead taken to the Holiday Inn Hotel Diner, one of the elite restaurants in Bremerton. After lunch, we were taken to East Bremerton and given a tour of some of the more exclusive neighborhoods, just in case we decided to relocate. At that time, I had limited knowledge of the layout of the city, and I had not thought about relocating, although the church did have a parsonage.

The parsonage was adjacent to the church building; it was a gray-and-white three-bedroom home, with a garage and a very large family room. We had liberal access to the home. We sometimes used it on the weekend, when there was an activity we had to attend, such as a business meeting, a church service, or civic affair. The church itself was a medium-size white building, with a seating capacity of about 125 people. A large basement contained restrooms for men and women, and it was used for Sunday school classes, general church meetings, and other fellowship activities. The church's cornerstone stated that the existing building had been constructed in 1945. Both buildings were stable structures, but the construction work had probably been done by volunteer labor supervised by self-proclaimed carpenters, bricklayers, plumbers, and painters. Except for the navy personnel, most of the church's male members worked for the Puget Sound Naval Shipyard as painters, plumbers, and sheet metal workers. One of the associate pastors was an excellent bricklayer and cement worker and owned his own company.

The church was located on Werner Road, and across from it was a very high hill of unimproved vacant land. Adjacent to the vacant land were two or three houses. The Reverend Henry Harris, one of the founders and an associate minister, and his family lived in one of the houses. Deacon Walter Frazier and his family occupied the other house.

Less than a block from Mount Zion was the Sinclair Missionary Baptist Church; we shared our church building with Sinclair Missionary Baptist for the Lent season, Easter sunrise service, and Christmas service.

During an afternoon worship service, Rev. C. A. Taylor, the pastor of Sinclair Missionary Baptist, welcomed me to the community, and we became very close friends. Pastor Taylor was a very mellow person who always had a cheerful word. One day, when we were talking about Mount Zion and Sinclair and the internal issues of the church, Pastor Taylor commented "Whenever one of Mount Zion's members' sneezes, a member of Sinclair gets a fever and a cold." Our congregations were that close, and Pastor Taylor and I remained friends and performed many services together until he retired.

As a new inexperienced pastor, I was quickly learning that some aspects of my personal situation, such as living in Tacoma, were not conducive to pastoring a group of people in Bremerton. The distance from Bremerton to Tacoma was about forty miles one way. I was also employed at Edmonds Community College to the north of Tacoma, and my duties required me to work at the Monroe Correctional Institution in Monroe, Washington. The congregation of Mount Zion was aware of this situation and agreed that my services would only be needed for Wednesday night Bible study and Sunday morning worship. Because of my inexperience and a lack of foresight by the board of deacons, we did not consider other additional pastor responsibilities, such as funerals, weddings, church business meetings, and supporting such organizations as the Ebenezer Baptist District Association and the North Pacific Baptist Convention. This demanding schedule required a great number of hours traveling between Monroe, Tacoma, and Bremerton, which placed extreme stress on my marriage.

The first year of my pastorate was harmonious. The first two major issues I had to deal with were the death of two church members and the resignation of a deacon. The first death was a middle-aged woman and choir member who was hospitalized the first month of my pastorate. The other was Deacon Frazier, who lived across the street from the church. He was a senior citizen and once was a very good softball player. His wife was deceased, and his adult daughters and teenage son, all of whom were adopted, lived with him. His death was a dreadful tragedy. His adopted son trapped him in a downstairs bedroom and set him and the house on fire. While I had observed my pastor officiating at a funeral, I had limited knowledge and preparation about how to visit a family at their home so my interaction with them was not very favorable. Deacon Frazier's daughters did not receive it well when my job prevented me from officiating at their father's funeral. They soon stopped attending Mount Zion, and I had very little contact with the family after the funeral.

As for the deacon who resigned, he was an elderly man who was a bit rough around the edges. His wife and daughter were very pleasant; both were very helpful within the church. His wife served as the church clerk and in the women's department. His daughter's marriage was the first official marriage ceremony I performed. This became another learning situation for me—the ceremony was enjoyable, but unfortunately, the marriage was short lived. As for the deacon, he was a bit controlling and narrow-minded about what he perceived as Christian values. The conflict that developed between us began when I requested that we place a Christmas tree in the sanctuary during the holiday season.

After the holidays were over, the deacon approached me to say, "Pastor, it is not right to bring a tree into the church." He made reference to a Bible verse and said, "Reverend, the Scriptures tell us not to bring a tree into the sanctuary. We should not have a tree in the church building during the holidays."

I said, "Deacon Jesse, I never read that in the Bible, and when you consider that our pews, podium, and most of the items in the church, including the building, all are made of wood from trees, it doesn't make sense." He looked puzzled and walked away. We never discussed the matter again, but he became the only member who ever withdrew membership by sending a letter to the church.

This event was the beginning of the storm that became for me a true case of being a sheep among wolves. When I was installed, I did not foresee that the sermon I preached on sheep among wolves would become a topic so relevant to my life. I believe one of the greatest kindnesses our Divine Creator gave to all humans was that He prevented us from having any concrete knowledge of our future.

We all have some type of personal trauma in our lives, but when you add to your life additional people with their issues, the tension mounts. When you have many people within a group who have personal issues, they infest the rest of the group with the toxic poisons of strife and division until the atmosphere resembles the storm clouds that appear before a hurricane.

Another issue that developed was that when I became the pastor of Mount Zion, the church was in the beginning phase of a building program. The poison of division developed because a portion of the congregation, especially the younger generation, was in favor of a new church building, while the older generation preferred to remain in the old one. Because I was not a permanent resident of Bremerton yet, I was unaware of what a territorial community it was. The initial families of the church, who came in the 1940s, had a different mind-set from those who joined in the 1960s and later. The older generation wanted things to remain as they were, while the younger generation wished for progress. Added to this mix was that Bremerton was a transient community. While the church had its permanent members, many of the members were U.S. Navy and civilian personnel; these families were excellent members, but except for the ones who chose to retire in Bremerton, they usually only remained for three years, so they were never fully committed to the church family. When you put all of those ingredients into what makes up a church family and then you have the vision for a new building program, the task can be overwhelming. Not to mention the unknown percentage—the silent, unknown disgruntled group waiting to rise up and attack.

The initial stage of the turmoil began probably after my second week as pastor. The church treasurer, a young officer in the U.S. Navy, approached me one Sunday after the worship service about having to issue checks to individuals not authorized by the former pastor or any of the church officers.

He said, "Pastor Rachal, I am concerned about issuing checks to individual members of the church without a signed voucher, and those individuals never report or produce a receipt of how the money was spent."

I asked, "Is there a voucher system?"

He replied, "No."

I asked, "Who is responsible for authorizing checks issued to members and for current expenses?"

The treasurer stated, "The chairman of the board of deacons and the chairman of the trustees is the same person."

I replied with surprise, "One individual is responsible for two critical leadership positions?" He just looked at me with a blank stare.

I informed him not to write any more checks until I had a meeting with the individual who held both positions. Then I scheduled a meeting with the board of deacons for that Saturday. That meeting turned out to be a bit "heated," but the individual was willing to give up the position of trustee chairperson because he had always been chairman of the board of deacons, and because he was a senior citizen and one of the church's founders, I did not challenge the issue. I thought, *Maybe he has been chairman of the board of deacons for too long.*

Because of my military background, for the past fifteen years, I had been in a leadership position. I was accustomed to giving orders and expecting them to be carried out, or the person would be subject to the Code of Military Discipline.

Civilian life and working with volunteers is a totally different set of rules and regulations, as well as there being an absence of any disciplinary action should the volunteer fail to carry out the request. I was quickly learning I had little or no recourse when things did not go according to my plans.

Another episode began to unfold during a conversation one Wednesday evening just before our weekly Bible study. I had arrived in Bremerton earlier than usual, so I was sitting outside of the church building enjoying the warm spring evening breeze.

One of our senior female members, a widower, Sister Betty Mae, arrived early that night. She had been a member of Mount Zion from its inception, and she was a member of the ushers board. Her parents, brothers, and sister had also been founders and longtime members of the church. Sister Betty Mae appeared to be very quiet, but that was a cover-up for her very sharp tongue.

When she and I began to talk about the Church Building Program, Sister Betty Mae stated, "My family is not in favor of a new building, and most of the old-timers are against relocating."

A bit startled by her statement, I responded, "Are you saying that a new building is not the desire of the majority of our members?"

She responded, "No, they're not in favor of it because my brother, Aaron, was the chairman of the board of trustees, but the former pastor pulled the rug from under him. My brother's plans were to remodel the existing building, but the pastor and the chairman of the board of deacons, Fally Tyson, changed those plans and did not inform my brother. The chairman of the board of deacons put some earnest money on a section of property off Sylvan Way in east Bremerton. Only a few of the members knew about this until it was stated in a general business meeting."

I was a bit startled and concerned by Sister Betty Mae's statement. While she, her sister, and two brothers, plus some of the other senior members, were not in one accord with the decision, the church membership was moving toward the construction of a new building. She and I had to discontinue our conversation at that point because other members were arriving for Bible study.

As I pondered the conversation I had with Sister Betty Mae on my drive back to Tacoma, I thought, *How do I handle this information? How much of it is true, and how much is just Sister Betty Mae's personal opinion? Was she seeking revenge because of what had happened to her brother?* And I wondered, *What is the true story about the purchase of the land, and why was this decision to purchase land not made in an official business meeting?* Over the next few months, I came to learn that this information was partially true, but Sister Betty Mae was also using it for self-serving purposes to get what she wanted in regards to the church.

I knew, as a new pastor, that my leadership skills would be in question for a time. While the members complimented me upon my preaching and teaching, I realized I was largely lacking knowledge on Baptist politics since I had been raised Catholic. I would soon have a rude awakening on this topic during one of our church business meetings.

I quickly realized the church's monthly business meetings were not well organized, and they were poorly attended. The dialogue among the members was limited, and when people attempted to express new ideas or simply their viewpoints, they were often verbally attacked by others. To try to remedy this situation and bring structure to how church business was conducted, I presented the church with copies of two books: *The Hiscox Guide for Baptist Churches* and *Robert's Rules of Parliamentary Procedures*.

I challenged the meeting moderator about how to open and close a meeting, and I emphasized the importance of keeping accurate records. For all meetings, I stated that there must always be a sign-in roster and an agenda.

I recommended that the church establish a voucher system for issuing funds from the church operation account. All church funds from any church auxiliary would be deposited into the church bank account. The church would maintain two accounts with a local bank, one for daily operating expenses, and one for the building fund.

I also discovered that the church did not have an official copy of the Mount Zion Missionary Baptist Church constitution and bylaws. I requested that an ad hoc committee be established to develop a church constitution and bylaws designed for the Mount Zion Missionary Baptist Church of Bremerton, Washington.

Mount Zion had other financial issues that included a mortgage on the existing church property and some of the funds designated for the mortgage having been used to purchase eleven acres of raw land with the vision to build a new church building. The church had later sold an acre of this land to the Government Housing Authority, which developed a senior citizen complex, Pinewood Manors, on Sylvan Way in Bremerton. We would need to get a handle on our financial issues if the church were to have a new building and stay out of the red.

Eventually, the church members decided that in order to raise money to build a new church on Sylvan Way, we would move out of our current building, tear it down, and sell the land. We would then rent space in another building while our new church was built. We followed through with these plans by tearing down the old church and renting space in the Masonic Temple. Plans went forward to sell the church's former property and build on the new property once the old property was sold, but things did not work out as planned from that point on.

My efforts had all been designed to bring order out of chaos and make the church's financial situation better while allowing all the members' voices to be heard. But not everyone appreciated these efforts. While I realized I could not please everyone, I assisted the congregation in doing what we believed the majority wanted and what would be best for Mount Zion Missionary Baptist Church.

Chapter 3

The Tragedy

The greatest tragedy is not failing, but giving up and not trying again—rest a while, but never quit.
—Pastor Sam Rachal, Jr.

Life in its fullness always presents some ups and downs. These ups and downs come in intervals of time that could last for days, weeks, or years. Serving as the shepherd of a Christian church body, there are times when life is very serene. The atmosphere feels like what a graceful great eagle must experience as it soars above the clouds in sweet serenity. But when devastating tragedy occurs, it can overwhelm your spiritual and moral values. Suddenly, the harmonious atmosphere is transformed into a raging storm, and you feel like you are on a cruise ship stranded at sea with thousands of passengers and no way back to shore.

The lessons to be learned during these trials and errors are to maintain a steadfast positive attitude with an inner assurance that along the journey of life, there will be trials and tribulations and also some victories, but each situation is short lived. The peaks and valleys of life's journey are training exercises that help to build character and develop wisdom that will strengthen our spiritual and moral values.

I once heard a senior pastor advising a group of young ministers with these words, "You are always in a storm, coming out of a storm, or about to enter a storm." In the most difficult times, however, steadfast perseverance, a positive attitude, and inner fortitude can turn a tragedy into a triumph. The Christian lifestyle defines such steadfastness as knowing the grace and mercy of the Lord. Great leaders, in both our spiritual and secular communities, are individuals who have endured more failures than successes; the key is to learn from the failures and to build on the successes.

One of the greatest tragedies in my life occurred during my tenure as pastor; this tragedy began to take shape in 1988.

By that time, the church had demolished our old Mount Zion building on Werner Road and relocated to the Masonic Temple while we tried to raise funds to build our new church on Sylvan Way. At this time, my salary as pastor, which had begun as $1,700 per month, was reduced by the church trustees, because our financial picture was upside down, to $700 per month. I agreed that the reduction was reasonable because of membership decline. Several members left because they were unhappy with the decision to tear down the old church, or they disagreed with the idea of worshiping God in a building associated with the Masons. The decline in church membership also resulted in reduced church funds.

Once the Mount Zion church family had relocated to the Masonic Temple, weekly church attendance had begun to drop down to an average of about sixty to seventy people, including members and visitors, with the usual monthly fluctuation due to our active duty navy members coming and going.

About this time, I talked with my family about becoming a full-time pastor. I do not fully recall their personal feelings about that option, but I knew they were not in love with the idea of moving to Bremerton.

My marriage had always been stormy. In the past we had experienced marriage problems, and our former pastors had given us some spiritual counseling, but we had never resolved the real-life issues that existed in our marriage, such as controlling the kind of anger that leads to rage and hatred. My life was always in a storm. We would find ourselves blaming or shaming one another, but with no concrete evidence and without any suggestions to resolve the situations that made us unhappy.

I needed advice about my marriage, but I truly felt alone and helpless because none of the previous advice I had received had been beneficial. I didn't know where to turn. Unfortunately, my former pastor, Reverend Bullock, had moved to California, so he was not available. Most of the pastors I knew were much younger than me, except for Reverend Brazill. I didn't have much confidence in pastors of other ethnicities because of the racial issues I had observed in Kitsap County. On several occasions, I had considered talking with the board of deacons at Mount Zion about my marriage, but I would change my mind, thinking, "Who cares about my personal life?"

Finally, I called Reverend Brazill and set up a meeting with him. He was very happy to offer me counsel. During our meeting, I explained to him the situation at the church. "My traveling time on the road is becoming difficult, and it hinders my duties as a pastor such as sermon preparation and teaching Bible study and Sunday school."

Reverend Brazill's suggestion was, "If you truly desire to improve as a pastor and to have your ministry grow, you must put the Lord's work first. Have you ever considered full-time service?"

My response was, "Yes." And I added, "The church is paying me a decent salary, yet our monthly expenses are consuming most of the money we have in the bank. Our major deficit is trying to build a new building on Sylvan Way, which is not going very well. Some of the property has been declared a wetland, so we cannot build on about an acre of the land." (This had been my first time hearing the term, *wetland*, which was a learning experience for me and the church members.)

Brother Brazill responded, "How much do you trust God? God will provide if you will commit to being a full-time pastor for Mount Zion."

I did not discuss anything about my marriage situation with Brother Brazill, including how my ex-wife was not pleased with me pastoring in Bremerton or that she did not want to live there. I'm not sure whether I stayed silent out of embarrassment or because of my previous experiences with other pastors. After all, I knew the Christian faith teaches fidelity, prayer, and commitment to marriage vows.

My session with Reverend Brazill was fruitful as it pertained to my ministry, but because of my failure to discuss my marriage issues, I left the session, thinking, *Why didn't I talk about my marriage?* This decision had not been very wise and would come back to haunt me when I decided to become a full-time pastor.

At the close of the school year in 1989, I resigned from my teaching position with Edmond Community College, and in September 1989, I became the full-time pastor at Mount Zion. I established my office hours, and I scheduled one day a week for hospital and home visits. I became a member of the Bremerton Ministerial Alliance and also a member of the Bremerton Lions Club.

During this time, I frequently visited Lil's Sandwich Shop in Bremerton for lunch. The restaurant was owned by Sister Wilson, one of the senior members of Mount Zion. Of course, the church pastor always ate free; my money was counterfeit at Lil's, and my sandwiches always had extra meat plus a healthy portion of potato chips. I met quite a few older members of the community there, and some of the city

The Tragedy

leaders would eat lunch at Lil's. The Job Service Center was across the street from the sandwich shop, so it brought in a crowd and made the restaurant a profitable enterprise.

My first few months as a full-time pastor were very lonely, except for a daily visit by Brother Crumpton, who always came by after picking up the church mail. I did not have a secretary, so I answered the phone and did a lot of reading for the first few months. Our Wednesday night Bible study was well attended, and I also started a noon-day prayer session for those senior members who did not want to travel after dark. Becoming a full-time pastor would develop into an emotional life-changing experience for me and the Mount Zion Baptist Church family.

The tragedy would involve the first family to leave the church after I became the pastor, the Peters family. To the Black community in Bremerton, Thomas and Cherry Peters and their three daughters were a living version of the television program, *Leave It to Beaver*. Both Thomas and Cherry were educators in the Central Kitsap School District. They were also musicians; Thomas Peters was a very articulate man with a beautiful tenor voice similar to that of Johnny Mathis, and he resembled movie star Billy Dee Williams. Cherry was a talented pianist who played classical, jazz, R & B, and of course, hymns and anthems.

The feud between the pastor and this family developed the first month after I was elected as pastor (we were still in the building on Werner Road). Information came to me through "the church grapevine" that Brother Peters was singing in one of the night clubs in Bremerton. Mistake number one for me was listening to such hearsay or gossip; that was my first lesson that you never act on hearsay or get involved in church gossip when you haven't seen the action and were not present yourself.

I requested that Brother Peters come to my office after Sunday morning service, and there I confronted him with the information. He did not deny it being true, but he replied, "I do not understand how this can affect my service to the church as a piano player."

I said, "Brother Peters, this type of behavior cannot continue. You must choose either to serve the Lord with your talents or to serve the secular world."

He departed my office with some visible anger. I must admit I did not make any attempt to verify the information. I could have been more diplomatic and tried to understand Brother Peters's position.

I cannot recall just how soon after this conversation the next event occurred. It happened one Sunday morning after worship service. Both Thomas and Cherry Peters requested a conversation with me. Sister Peters did most of the talking.

She stated, "Pastor, you cannot talk with my husband when I am not present; we are a team, and you should have waited until we were both present to discuss this issue." She was crying and very upset.

I was a bit startled by her statement and concerned about her emotional state. I said, "Sister Peters, this issue involved only Brother Peters. I do not understand why I had to postpone the conversation until you were present or why I needed your permission to speak with your husband."

Sister Peters stated, "We are a team, and we do things together. If you do not want my husband to play the piano, I will not play either."

I replied, "This has nothing to do with your playing for the church, and you are not singing in a nightclub."

After some discussion, I discovered how protective Sister Peters was of her spouse. The conversation began to escalate, so I suggested we terminate the meeting until a future time.

That meeting never occurred, and the family was absent from the church for at least three weeks. After that, Sister Peters and her three girls returned and began to attend regularly, but Brother Peters only came on special occasions to assist his wife with the music. Brother Peters and I were always cordial with each other following this incident, but we never developed a wholesome or harmonious relationship.

Not long after she returned to church, Sister Peters approached me again. She asked me to meet with her for marriage counseling. I was surprised, but I could see she was a woman with a sincere desire to have a wholesome and loving family. She was also a cheerful person who was easy to talk with, and she had been raised under the Baptist persuasion, had a sincere respect for her pastor, and was very loyal to the church. She also knew, because I had informed the church, that I had a certificate in marriage and family counseling.

While I was willing to help Sister Peters, I was surprised that her husband was not included in the request for marriage counseling, so I said to her, "Sister Peters, it would be more profitable if Thomas were part of our counseling session, especially since we shall be discussing issues about your marriage."

She stated, "I am afraid my husband has not gotten over the first conversation both of you had, so he would not be open to counseling from you."

I had been previously warned and cautioned, "Never meet alone with females." Also, I had been warned that "it can sometimes be harmful to counsel a member of the church because you might make a statement in a sermon or when you are teaching that sounds exactly like what was discussed in a counseling session." I do believe this advice has merit, but it is very difficult not to give guidance when a church member requests help. So I conceded to give her counsel.

For a short time, I was able to use one of the offices at the Pinewood Manor Apartments, so during that initial session, we were in a private place. Soon after when the church moved to the Masonic Temple, I shared an office, so most of the sessions were in the general meeting room downstairs. Because of the confidentiality involved, I cannot disclose the contents of our sessions, yet as a general statement, I can say that most marriage issues develop within the arena of communication about such things as honesty, finances, and infidelity; all of these problems result from poor and immature communication.

During this time, the Rachals and Peters family developed a good relationship; the family visited our home several times on the weekends. It was not unusual for me to have lunch with Sister Peters, especially on Saturdays after meetings with the church leaders. Our relationship, however, gradually shifted to where I realized the counseling session and lunch date were becoming more about our friendship than her marriage and family.

During a business meeting in 1990, I informed the congregation that I would be moving to Bremerton. A church family wanted me to live in their home while they were away for several months. Relocating to Bremerton would relieve my drive between Tacoma and Bremerton, and it would also relieve some of the storms in my marriage that was now falling apart. We were having many arguments about finances, disciplining our children, and church attendance. My wife was always more comfortable in a church that was of mixed cultures, but I was not. When we had arrived in Tacoma, Washington, we joined an Independent Baptist Church. I was not very happy in this situation, especially since it was at a time when I truly felt a special call on my life. I then joined Bethlehem in Tacoma, but I do not recall whether my family ever joined Bethlehem. There was very little respect for Black leadership in the spiritual or secular community in my home. Consequently, my decision to relocate to Bremerton was a relief from years of emotional pressure and anxiety. The relief was short term, however, because a few weeks later, my wife called to tell me she was having surgery. "The doctor recommended that I have a hysterectomy, so you need to move back home to care for me," she said.

I told her, "I will come back, but as soon as you're better, I am moving back to Bremerton." And I added, "I will be filing for a divorce because, from my perspective, the marriage is over."

I did move back to Tacoma to care for my wife, and about ninety days later, I returned to Bremerton. At that time, one of the church members offered to let me live in a room in her home until I could rent an apartment. She and her husband lived alone and had a large home in East Bremerton. At that point, I was happy for a temporary solution since my divorce was in its early stages, and my financial situation had me living paycheck to paycheck. Because of its financial difficulties, the church had decided to reduce my salary, and my military retirement pay was not sufficient to meet all of my obligations. To supplement my income, I secured a job as a drug and alcohol counselor with the Agape Unlimited Drug and Alcohol Program. I often felt that the years I worked at Agape were more therapeutic for me than for some of the clients I counseled. It made me realize my situation was trivial in comparison to some of my clients who were confronted with incarceration, divorce, children in foster homes, bankruptcy, and homelessness because of their chemical addictions. It was an emotional relief for me to believe each day that I may have helped a person to stay clean from chemicals and start a chemical-free lifestyle.

While my life should have felt like it was taking a turn for the better, my pending divorce and my friendship with the church piano player,

Sister Peters, was leading to gossip in the church community. One Sunday, during a morning service, there were derogatory statements made doing service as I preached by some members. At the conclusion of my sermon, I extended the "invitation to discipleship," a spiritual challenge to the unsaved to become a member of the body of Christ, to join Mount Zion Baptist Church, or just come for prayer. I closed the service with a prayer and went downstairs to change my clothes.

I finally went home, and shortly after, a couple of deacons came over to discuss the derogatory statements that were being made during the service. It was stated that some members were threatening to leave the church or that the pastor needed to leave.

The following week, things were a bit tense. The service went as usual, but I was embarrassed and a little shaken because of the previous incident. The whispers and innuendoes about Sister Peters and me were moving fast through Bremerton. Soon, the president of African American ministers requested my presence at a meeting. The pastors in attendance were from the Apostolic and Church of God in Christ denominations (the names of those ministers are not included to protect the integrity of the Christian church). They attempted to censure me about the gossip, which was just that—community gossip that Sister Peters and Pastor Rachal were having an affair. I challenged them with a verse from Scripture about gossip: "And beside they learn to be idle, and not only idle but also gossips and busybodies, saying things which they ought not" (1 Timothy 5:13 NKJV). Another minister challenged the audience about charging a pastor without the witness of one or more clergy. When I had first arrived in Bremerton, Pastor Taylor had informed me that one of the ministers who had called this meeting had been charged with having keys to the homes of some of the single women in his congregation. When Pastor Taylor and I had confronted him, he had denied the rumors. Now I believed he saw this situation as payback time for me. When I addressed his previous behavior during this meeting, those supporting him said his behavior was in the past and not the purpose of this discussion. The meeting was quickly terminated without being brought to any real conclusion.

My divorce proceedings continued, which was both hurtful and embarrassing. I was being harassed by a collection agency trying to make me pay for a ring that I didn't purchase. Furthermore, my divorce attorney was not very sharp; sometimes I wondered whose side he was on. Because of my military service, most of my legal problems were transacted through the Judge Advocate Office of Military Affairs. My divorce became final in May 1990.

I thought I was over a hurdle then, but in November or December of that same year, the church moderator, Deacon William Jones, called me one Thursday evening. "Pastor," he told me, "the church members have requested a church business meeting for this Saturday. The meeting's purpose is to request your resignation. If you choose not to resign, the membership will vote by secret ballot whether to remove you as pastor of the Mount Zion Missionary Baptist Church of Bremerton, Washington."

I was devastated by this news, but I managed to say, "Deacon Jones, I do not intend to resign, and if I am voted out as the pastor of Mount Zion, I am still a member of the church, so I will be at worship service on Sunday morning."

I do not remember very much after the call from Brother Jones. I felt shaken, yet I knew resignation was not an option for me. I also knew the Lord would have the last word.

I did not get much sleep Thursday night. On Fridays, I only worked a half day at Agape. Friday morning was about our client caseload and some in-house training about new and old policies and procedures for handling chemically addicted clients.

On Saturday morning, I took a walk and did a lot of praying. I thought about my work in the ministry and my dedication to the Mount Zion church family. When I had arrived at Mount Zion, the congregation had a permanent church building; now we were worshipping our Lord in the Masonic Temple. I knew the church had financial problems, and the reduction of my salary was not a major issue for me yet, but I truly believed that part of the reason for the reduction of my salary was to force my resignation. During a church business meeting, I had informed the members that I had no intentions of resigning even if the church failed to pay me any salary.

I can clearly remember leaving my apartment that Saturday evening. I did not want to be late, so I arrived at the building about 5:45 p.m.; the business meeting was at 6:00 p.m. A few people had arrived early for the meeting, and most of them greeted me. Then I went into my office and gathered my thoughts, taking a few deep breaths to relax. I was feeling nervous, but I thought, *Lord, if the vote to remove me as pastor is approved, I will be in the Masonic Temple building tomorrow as a member of Mount Zion.*

The tension in the meeting room was obvious; the people were silent, although some whispered among themselves. I could identify, by facial looks and group seating, most of the members who wanted me to resign. Those I felt would support me appeared to be together as their own group.

It seemed like an eternity before the moderator called the meeting to order. He followed the normal procedure; one deacon read from the Scripture and another prayed.

The Tragedy

Then the moderator addressed me, "Pastor Sam Rachal, Jr., it is the request of some of the members that you resign as the pastor of Mount Zion Missionary Baptist Church of Bremerton. What is your statement to the church body?"

I stood very stoic and, with diplomacy, said, "I do not intend to resign or move my membership from the Mount Zion Missionary Baptist Church." I sat down and the moderator spoke to the audience.

"Since Pastor Rachal refuses to resign, what is the church's pleasure?"

One member stood up and made the request, "Can I ask Pastor Rachal a question?"

The moderator said yes, and the member asked, "Pastor Rachal, is it true that you and Sister Peters are having an affair?"

I stood and said, "That is not the purpose of this meeting, and I will not answer questions about my personal life."

Another member stood up and made a motion. "I move that the church vote by secret ballot to remove Pastor Sam Rachal, Jr. as pastor of the Mount Zion Missionary Baptist Church."

A voice in the audience said, "I second the motion."

The moderator responded, "It has been moved and properly seconded that the church vote by secret ballot for or against the motion."

The moderator added, "Call the question. Call the question. Call the question? There being no question, all in favor of the motions, vote yes."

"Yes," the audience responded.

"All opposed," the moderator continued, "vote no." None were opposed.

The moderator declared, "So moved."

The church secretary handed out blank sheets of paper, and the church voted. The deacons picked up the votes. The moderator and a few chosen members left the room to count the ballots. As I recall, there was total silence in the room. Between the time when the group left the room to count the ballots and their return, there appeared to be time without end.

A few minutes later, the moderator returned to the meeting with a slip of paper. He paused and read the results, concluding, "Pastor Rachal shall remain as pastor."

I was relieved to remain as pastor, yet I knew my future looked very bleak—some of the members had already left the church, plus a young minister had joined the church who had become my major enemy. He had helped to spread the gossip about the affair with Sister Peters and was attempting to start his own church. However, neither he nor the church he began lasted very long because of some issues he had with women and taking funds from the church. According to public records, he was later arrested in Tacoma for child molestation.

Pictures

Top: Sam Rachal, Jr., Altar Boy
Bottom: Sam Rachal, Jr., Enlists in army, 1954

Top: Sam Rachal, Jr., Vietnam, 1967-1968
Center Left: Sam Rachal, Jr., Vietnam, 1969-1970
Center Right: Sam Rachal, Jr., El Paso, Texas, 1972
Bottom: Cherry and Sam Rachal, Jr., Wedding

Top: Sam Rachal, Jr. and his daughter
Center: Sam Rachal, Jr. and his sons
Bottom: *Papa's El Camino* painted by Hasaan Kirkland

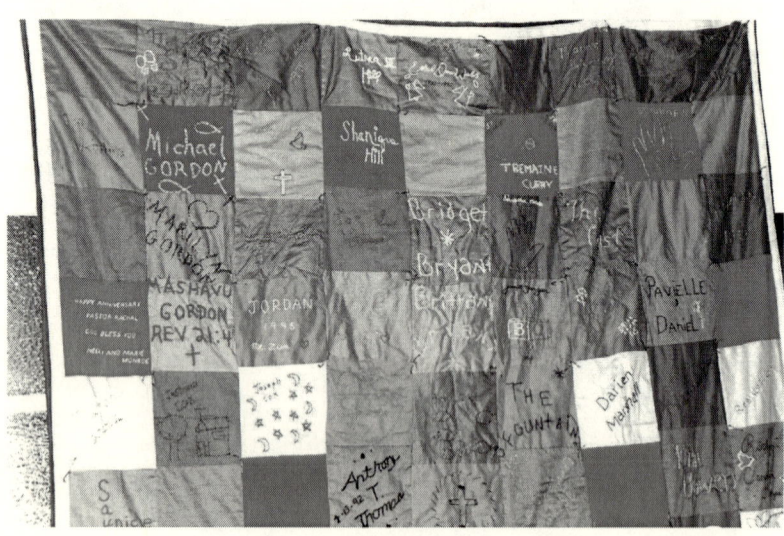

Top: Mt. Zion Missionary Baptist Church, Bremerton, Washington
Bottom: Blanket-Gift from Junior Church members.

Chapter 4

The Road Back from Failure

*It is very difficult to be humble if you are always successful,
so God chastises us with failure at times in order to humble us,
to keep us in a state of humility.*
—D. Martyn Lloyd-Jones (1899-1981)

One of the most prominent people in the New Testament is Peter. He became the cornerstone and leader of the twelve apostles after Jesus's ascension into heaven. This stalwart figure of the New Testament, however, knew failure. When Jesus was arrested and tried before Pontius Pilate, Peter, who had vowed to be Jesus's source of stability, failed the test. When questioned by a young lady whether he was one of Jesus's followers, Peter denied any personal relationship with the prophet who claimed to be the son of God. Soon after, Peter repented, and he became the chief spokesman for the Christian faith; in time, he would die a martyr's death, choosing to be crucified upside down because of his humility and his belief that he did not deserve to die the same way as his Lord. Peter is an example of how God uses frail, sinful human beings as instruments to carry out His purpose to evangelize to all people.

Knowing I had failed, I did not forget that God has used failure for good in the past. Such was my mind-set after going through a divorce and nearly being removed from my role as pastor. I knew I now had to lead the congregation, including moving us into a permanent building for worship and by serving the larger Bremerton community.

The Saturday night after it was voted that I remain as pastor of Mount Zion, I was finally able to get some sleep. However, I knew that the future of my ministry would be unstable for a while until the gossip settled. In the end, I trusted that people would be forgiving, and I knew that with most issues, time heals all wounds, even if the mental anguish during the healing process can be horrible. During this time, I moved into a relatively inexpensive one-bedroom apartment located in Manette, a small suburb of Bremerton.

The church's membership had now dwindled down to about twelve to eighteen faithful families, but those who remained knew about my divorce and were very supportive of my ministry. Most of these families had been members of Mount Zion when I became pastor, and they all served in key roles within the church body, such as deacons and deaconesses, church moderator, trustees, finance secretary, and church clerk. The membership always included many military families stationed at U.S. Navy Bangor and Puget Sound Naval Base. These families, and a few later additions, would become the cornerstone of the Mount Zion Missionary Baptist Church. Thus, collectively, the church family began a period of recovery.

Many of our members had belonged to other denominations before arriving in Bremerton. Some had been Methodists or part of the church of God in Christ. A few were former Catholics, so they could relate to me as a pastor who had also once been a Catholic. Nevertheless, we all had some learning to do about what we believed and why we practiced our religious faith as Baptists. Some had been baptized but never knew why baptism was essential or the biblical principles of first, salvation by grace, followed by baptism by immersion.

My initial baptism into the Baptist faith had not explained to me the biblical perspective of Baptism by immersion. During my time attending an Independent Baptist Church in Texas and Alaska, my family and I were taught and participated in learning God's plan of salvation. In Paul's letter to the Romans, Paul describes humanity's separation from God by sin and God's method of redemption—salvation by grace. The Independent Baptist churches define this process toward salvation as the "Romans' Road."

Many of the members of Mount Zion had never heard or learned these Scripture verses, or they had limited knowledge about evangelism—going into the community to share with the unsaved and the unchurched how they can come to know Jesus as Lord and Savior.

Teaching this principle of salvation was a major task when I began my ministry at Mount Zion. It was very difficult because some of our older members resisted any new teachings about the Bible. I truly believe they had heard some of the information in the past, but they had not grasped its true meaning. Most of the people who were under thirty-five years of age were eager to learn more about a personal relationship with Jesus Christ.

The first Sunday of each month during the worship service, the congregation observed the Lord's Supper. It was an open communion service, and all could partake in eating the bread and drinking the wine (grape juice). I was shocked to learn that most of our older generation thought that their observance of the Lord's Supper ensured them a place in heaven. My task was to teach them that the ritual of baptism and observance of the Lord's Supper were not equal to salvation and a ticket into heaven; instead, it was because of our salvation by grace that we observed these rituals, in obedience to the command given by Jesus Christ. The apostle Paul had explained this matter very clearly when he wrote: "For this reason many are weak and sick among you, and many died" in reference to people observing the Lord's Supper in vain, not recognizing the significance of Christ's death, burial, and resurrection (1 Corinthians 11:30 NKJV). Mankind's salvation is by grace, not from works so that no one should boast. Jesus commanded his followers to observe the Lord's Supper in simple obedience to His command.

Serving in my first tenure as a church pastor, I was still in the learning stage about being a pastor, but my knowledge of the Bible and my abilities to teach biblical principles such as the interpretation or exegesis of the Scriptures was a surprise to many people, especially since these were seasoned Christian seniors who had grown up in church-going families. The issue was that some had never learned the fundamentals of what Baptists believe or the biblical support for those beliefs. I had previously heard the phrase "reading your people," but I had not given this viewpoint much thought; now this concept became very important as my ministry developed. Every individual can be compared to reading an unfamiliar story. Some stories are easy reading, and you can grasp the plot after the first reading, but others must be reread before you understand the plot and how it fits into the outcome. Notwithstanding, these senior members were very supportive of the church and my ministry. So I had to ask myself, "How do I present this information without creating division or putting my congregation on the defensive about what they already have learned about Christianity?"

Most people, I believe, do not enjoy reading, except perhaps reading the local newspaper or a magazine. People must realize, however, that in order to gain a true understanding of the Bible, extensive study is required. Most people will simply accept what is stated by the pastor, which I do not believe is healthy. I began to teach the members of Mount Zion to read, study the Scriptures for their own edification, and also to do some outside reading such as a biblical commentary with a moderate viewpoint or read some of the sacrosanct writings by biblical scholars.

The Lord had provided wonderful people to worship at Mount Zion, and some were eager to learn. One dilemma, however, that troubled my spirit was the number of transient people—navy families and civilian navy employees—who joined the church; it became very apparent that most of them would be relocated after eighteen months or three years, although some retired and remained at Mount Zion. They provided outstanding service by their attendance, financial giving, and leadership skills. So it was heartbreaking for the church family when they had to relocate to another duty station. Over a twenty-year period, the number of these families who passed through Mount Zion may have been in the hundreds. Yet Mount Zion was truly blessed because today we have members throughout the United States and foreign lands who still call Mount Zion their church home.

Still, I felt guiding these people was a great burden on me and the church. The issue tugged at my heartstrings for some time until I began to question God about this burden. I asked, "Lord, why did you place me in this community as my first ministry?"

When I had acknowledged my call to the ministry, I had envisioned myself as an evangelist. My home base would be at the Bethlehem church in Tacoma, and I would go around the country preaching revivals. But that was my vision, not the Lord's. As the undershepherd of God's people, in time, I found that being the pastor at Mount Zion, despite the ups and downs and issues, would be a very rewarding and lifelong service.

Because I enjoyed teaching the Bible and also church administration, I began to read and research information about church organization. I ordered a five-volume set of books about church management and

Christian growth and leadership. I also read several books about Baptist churches and a pastor's duties and responsibilities. One book I am very happy I purchased early in my ministry was *The Minister's Service Manual* by Samuel Ward Hutton. This manual is an excellent guide for performing funerals, marriages, the dedication of infants, and for advice on visiting the sick in their homes or in the hospital. The manual also offers some excellent suggestions about records that ministers should keep and having a personal calendar.

My first experience officiating at a marriage ceremony was for a young lady whose family were members of the church. At that time, Mount Zion was still worshipping at our church building on Werner Road. The ceremony moved very smoothly with only a few small glitches. At my next marriage ceremony, however, I made a grave mistake. By then, the church had relocated to the Masonic Temple. The service went well, although as always, the service did not start on time, but after the ceremony, I requested that the bride, groom, and the two witnesses come to my office to sign the marriage license, only to find out that the couple had failed to secure a marriage license. What a fiasco that was! And a great learning experience for me. Never again did I make that mistake. I learned that the law required a three-day waiting period from the time the license was issued until any marriage ceremony could be performed. My firm policy became the following: first, we engage in a conversation about marriage—marriage is for mature adults, unconditional love is the foundation, how the relationship develops after the marriage vows and how divorce destroys both parties; second, the couple must have in their possession the marriage license before any marriage ceremony.

Serving as a full-time pastor allowed me to become totally involved in ministry. It was the fulfillment of Reverend Brazill's statement that my ministry would grow and my spiritual life blossom as I came to understand that "true commitment means serving the Lord full-time; it is not just an eight-hour job; the true servant is always on duty." I found this statement to be fruitful and very valuable. I truly learned that "Where your treasure is, there your heart will be also." Serving as the shepherd of God's people became my lifelong purpose.

One of the first ministries I reestablished as a full-time pastor was noon-day prayer hour. Some of our seniors preferred not to drive after dark, and for others, this time provided an option to be in a prayer service during their lunch hour. I was also a member of the Bremerton Ministerial Alliance, which met once a month. I appreciated being part of this organization because I gained some valuable information about ministry from various cultures. The Alliance's members had a mixture of liberal, conservative, and middle-of-the-road perspectives about worshiping God and their relationships with church members. This participation became a rich and rewarding experience for me.

The African American Ministers had established their own alliance, but it was a dysfunctional one. A young female minister, who had been assigned to the Ebenezer Methodist Church in Bremerton, was interested in revitalizing the African American Alliance, so we did so, giving it a new title: Bremerton African American Ministerial Alliance (BAAMA). Today, this organization continues to be very active in the community.

I also became involved in the local community's National Association for the Advancement of Colored People, (NAACP) Bremerton's chapter. At that time, a group of active young Blacks also organized a civic group: People Working Together for Ethnic Reality (POWER). It was very apparent at this time that racial unrest was affecting our children in the school system and the people in our community. Within Kitsap County, Blacks were unrepresented in the political arena, and their leadership was limited within the employment industry and the school system. Altogether, there was only one Black judge, two attorneys (who arrived after I did), and Kitsap County had one minority deputy sheriff and the City of Bremerton had maybe two minorities serving on the police force. A Black male served as the acting captain on the Bremerton police force, but that was very short lived. The school districts of Bremerton, Central Kitsap, and North and South Kitsap contained less than twenty Black teachers. As for businesses, I was only aware of Blacks owning one barbershop and beauty shop. For the most part, Blacks only owned their own homes, churches, and one social club, the Hickory House. Since I had become pastor of Mount Zion Missionary Baptist Church, some limited economic and social changes had occurred, but the African American population in Kitsap County remained far removed from having a viable impact on the political and social issues that affected our people and all people within Kitsap County.

Meanwhile, the years the church family worshiped in the Masonic Temple located on Burrell Street in West Bremerton were very difficult. The building was red brick and probably built sometime before 1940. The building was constructed with three levels, with ample space for offices and bathrooms. The kitchen was large, but all the plumbing and fixtures in both the kitchen and bathrooms were from the 1940s or 1950s. On the third floor was a large auditorium room, which adequately housed about one hundred people and was used by the lodge members for their meetings. However, because of the stigma attached to the Prince Hall Masons organization and some of its extracurricular activities, some people preferred not to worship in the building. To keep everyone happy, we used a local school's auditorium for our service for a while, but that was short lived; the task of setting up and disassembling and the storage of furniture became a burden, and no one was willing to do it every week. Churches have an unwritten principle that 20 percent of the people do 80 percent of the work. Mount Zion's Board of Trustees tried to work with another organization for space, but the cost and the building's design just were not conducive for our church worship service. The Masonic Temple, therefore, became the most efficient place for the church's needs.

Our members then agreed to use the Masonic Temple as our place of worship, but only temporarily. The church used the upstairs for Sunday School and worship service. The lower level's large room was used for Youth Sunday School and Junior Church Service. The kitchen was a valuable asset because during the Junior Church Service, there was time for snacks; also, when the church conducted an afternoon service, such as church or pastor anniversaries or ushers annuals, the kitchen was used to prepare the food, and the area downstairs was large enough to set up tables and chairs for our guests to enjoy a home-cooked meal.

The church had ample chairs, tables, office equipment, and pulpit furniture to use in the building. And while the Masons used the building and the Blacks in government had the office across from mine, most of our members were acquainted with the government officials and Mason members, so we all got along, and our activities did not conflict.

Even when people know a situation is not permanent, after a while, they will relax and accept the situation, which can be good and bad—good because people appear happy, but bad because people become complacent and forget the vision of a church building. The property on Sylvan Way was still a feasible objective for building a new building. However, the income of tithes and offerings was barely sufficient to meet the church's needs, so to build a new building and continue paying the mortgage on the Sylvan Way property made Mount Zion's church family feel less than optimistic. However, my goal remained to get our church family back into a permanent residence.

Added to the pressure at this time, my son, Sam Rachal III, had a terrible automobile accident that nearly took his life and the life of a young man who was a passenger in the vehicle. Sam III had been driving under the influence of alcohol. The vehicle was destroyed, and my son was hospitalized for over three weeks. The passenger was hurt, but he recovered. My son had a numbers of cuts and bruises, but he came out of the accident on the positive side. His employer helped by paying his court and rehabilitation treatment fees. Thanks to God, this accident became a life-changing experience for my son. After that, he quit using any mind-altering substances. Today, he lives in Oregon, has purchased a home, and is employed as a cable splicer for a telephone company.

Another overwhelming event that occurred during this time was that my daughter, Jarutha Rena, was diagnosed with multiple sclerosis (MS). A few weeks after she was diagnosed with MS, she developed pneumonia and went into a very deep depression. When her brother Sam III (nicknamed Frankie) stopped in for a visit, he found her alone in her apartment and dehydrated almost to the point of being in a coma. She was in and out of the hospital after this event, and eventually, she was placed in several rehabilitation centers. Jarutha's major problem, in my opinion, was that she had refused to accept her situation, so she tried to maintain the lifestyle of a person in perfect health. Also, while I had known about her use of marijuana, she soon graduated to crack cocaine and other streets drugs. Her death in 1999 from her disease was a horrifying experience for me; parents never envision burying their children. Jarutha was a daddy's girl and the princess in our home when she was a child. While my divorce had put a strain on my relationship with my sons, Jarutha never changed toward me; she could do no wrong in my eyes, and I had no flaws in her eyes. My daughter's death still causes me much guilt and questions linger in my mind: Why did this illness have to attack my only beautiful daughter? Why did she get involved in the drug culture, and why did she choose never to marry but have a live-in boyfriend?

Such events caused me to reflect upon and appreciate the biblical philosophy behind praying, "Give us this day our daily bread." We must learn to live one day at a time. As I said before, it is a true blessing that we do not have knowledge of the future.

A challenging question I found myself asking about all the difficulties I underwent during these years was, "Is God's spiritual discipline a punishment or training, or are the two working in harmony?" I believe the two do work in harmony, but the process is stressful and emotionally draining because of the guilt and sorrow that taunt your soul during the teaching period. God's school of instruction is not a pass/fail; it is a lifelong process of helping an individual to develop humility—a humble spirit. Dying to self is the most difficult task because the self is always in denial of the truth, and the self rationalizes bad behavior. As humans, we tend to worship the creation more than the Creator. During the training period, God tries to help us to remove the focus off ourselves. A personal death to self still leaves us alive, but with learnt self-control and long suffering.

Worshipping at the Masonic Temple was, for me, as the pastor, the thorn in the flesh. Whatever happened, good or evil, the pastor can be seen as the flaw. In my case, I was perceived as the one responsible for destroying the old church building before building a new one, which may have added to the problems that led to the accusations about my infidelity and my divorce. I knew I had to climb out of this self-made condemnation, but I felt that for me to do so would require a miracle, and I lacked the mental awareness to know where to start.

What I did know, which became my security blanket, was that I was called by God to work for Jesus. I knew that my mission in the world was to preach and teach the Word of God. To evangelize to the lost using the eternal word of God is to promote truth without error. I knew God had not anointed me to be successful but to be faithful and to trust in Him, for the Word says, "Humble yourself before a Holy God and He will exalt you." (James 4:10) The more I focused on the will of God instead of my own human desires, the more I developed a humble spirit, which became my Rock of Salvation. I had failed God, but I knew the God I served could not fail. A humble spirit was all God required. Do all you can do and leave the rest to God.

Sometimes I still ask myself, "What if the building program I was introduced to at the beginning of my ministry at Mount Zion had been successful? Then what would have been the results of my ministry?" Those questions will never be answered, yet I believe in the providence of God. My failure to achieve material success for our church brought our church family spiritual success. The lesson I learned was the following: It was never about me; it was, and still is, all about God and how God can turn failure into a blessing and promote a humble spirit.

I was not to enjoy a new church building but to learn a greater lesson about ministry: "True Christian service is humility."

Humility, the place of entire dependence in God, is, from the very nature of things, the first duty and the highest virtue of the creature, and the root of every virtue.
—Andrew Murray

Chapter 5

Failure is Not Final

It's okay to fail, but do not quit; the resilient spirit rises up from a failure.
—Pastor Sam Rachal, Jr.

The sanctity of marriage has always been viewed as special by humanity. While this position about the holiness of marriage may vary from person to person, according to his or her spiritual values, most individuals yearn for a special someone to whom they can commit and with whom they can enjoy their life together. Those individuals with a Christian heritage accept the biblical concept about how marriage first began, following the creation and God creating the first human, Adam.

And the Lord God said, "It is not good that man should be alone; I will make him a helper comparable to him." Out of the ground, the Lord God formed every beast of the field and every bird of the air and brought them to Adam to see what he would call them. And whatever Adam called each living creature, that was its name. So Adam gave names to all cattle, to the birds of the air, and to every beast of the field.

But for Adam, there was not found a helper comparable to him.

And the Lord God caused a deep sleep to fall on Adam, and he slept; and He took one of his ribs, and closed up the flesh in its place.

Then the rib which the Lord God had taken from man He made into a woman, and He brought her to the man.

And Adam said:

> This is now bone of my bones
> and flesh of my flesh;
> she shall be called Woman,
> because she was taken out of Man."
> Therefore a man shall leave his father and mother and be
> joined to his wife, and they shall become one flesh.
> (Genesis 2:18-24, NKJV)

Whether or not we accept the biblical version of creation, we all enjoy the benefits of creation, and many unite as husband and wife and enjoy the fellowship of marriage and family. In most cases, two mature individuals, male and female, recite their marriage vows of commitment and are united in marriage. A covenant is made between a man and woman when the two recite and agree to the vow, "until death do us part." The covenant means that the two individuals become one.

A violation of the covenant agreement means that which was once united is divided and becomes two disjointed bodies enduring physical and emotional separation. Their visible appearance may be of two whole people, but unseen perhaps by human eyes are two emotionally hurting people who are internally broken. A divorce destroys more than a married couple; children, if there are any, are hurt, and the pain also extends to both biological families and some friends.

During the initial phase of my divorce, I had developed the attitude "I do not need any company to live in torment and daily emotional anxiety." The fallout from a divorce was just additional torment and daily emotional pain. It was a mixture of grief and joy over newfound freedom—an emotional roller coaster.

After our children were out of the home, my marriage, which had always consisted of constant bickering, became a much more hostile environment than when the children were growing up. After the divorce, I was haunted by the humiliating gossip and the agonizing fallout of the divorce settlements. What I thought would be liberation became aggravation. I had my freedom, but divorce means just that—separation—from my ex-wife and my personal property. I was emotionally exhausted. The financial cost and the division of property promoted anger and disappointment in me.

Everything my ex-wife and I had worked and struggled to accumulate, we allowed three uninvolved people, two lawyers and a judge, to divide as they saw fit. Two emotionally hurting, angry, disappointed individuals allowed the justice system to decide their future. There are no winners in a divorce. First, because your decisions are clouded by frustration and unsympathetic anger, you tend to make quick emotionally driven decisions. I am a living example that emotionally hurting people can make unwise choices that have devastating consequences.

Was I receptive to any sound advice? Probably not, and chances are I probably would have refused any. My mind-set was simply "I want out of this marriage."

Months later, I realized I had made some unwise choices, not about the divorce, but the process. I had not thought through what I was about to do, and what the results would mean. Months later, I was learning some harsh lessons as I went through frequent mental anguish. Aside from the financial loss, divorce is a harsh reality that two people made vows—a commitment—that they truly did not understand. The divorce rate in our society proves the necessity of premarriage counseling and that marriage is for mature adults.

During a divorce, blaming and shaming the other party and denying one's personal failure is not helpful. Anger is prevalent. Gradually, it is replaced by acceptance, and then the long tedious journey of recovery begins—and recovery is endless. Throughout the recovery, people continue to question themselves, and they must confront their own selfishness. They may believe they did the right things previously, such as create a sound financial base for their marriage, were a supporting spouse and parent but deep down, selfishness destroys a marriage. It takes two to join in matrimony and two to destroy the vows of marriage. No one destroys a marriage alone; each person is partially responsible.

After my divorce, the reality of my failure set in. First, because of my spiritual values, I felt I had failed God. Then I believed I had failed myself and my family, and also my church family, which enhanced my personal guilt.

Finally, I began to recover when I was able to tell myself, "It is okay to fail because *failure is not final*."

When we can muster the courage to recover from any blunder, we learn to put into practical application one of the principles we learn from the Lord's Prayer, to live by our daily needs, "Give us this day our daily bread."

The first step of my recovery became the hardest: forgiving myself. Forgiveness can be difficult because the mind remembers every detail that the inner person would like to forget.

I believed in God's unlimited forgiveness, and I learned that the people who love you are there to support you as you move forward. Thus, I made "failure is not final" my personal proverb to live by.

After my divorce, the church family began to rebound. The gossip, finger-pointing, and degrading stares began to subside. Those who called for my removal as pastor relocated their membership. The young minister who was a wolf in sheep's clothing began his own fellowship, which lasted only about ninety days.

At this time, the deacons and their wives requested a meeting with Cherry Peters and me to discuss the church's future and my future as its pastor and a member. The meeting was cordial. Cherry and I were honest about the fact that we had been dating and about our personal outings in the public eye, knowing that our behavior had dishonored our Lord, our personal integrity, and the reverence of the church. The group agreed that our Lord forgives sins, but those sins must be confessed and repented; therefore, we needed to repent, accept God's forgiveness, and learn to forgive ourselves. The group did not suggest or infer that Cherry and I needed to address the church body concerning what was discussed during the meeting.

The healing process was not easy. Both Cherry and I needed some emotional healing. Both of us had experienced a difficult marriage and divorce, and we were attempting to rebuild our lives. The church body also needed to experience the healing process.

While the church body did not expect a public confession, Cherry and I knew the right thing to do was to marry or for one of us to leave the church. We were sure neither of us had any desire to leave Mount Zion. We believed in forgiveness, and we knew some would forgive, but not all.

Additional fallout from a divorce is the individual personal knowledge of unrighteous behavior. Spiritually, the person knows he or she is forgiven, but replacing guilt with an acceptance of personal forgiveness is a daily process. The other part of the healing process was living with rejection. The comforting part came from those who continued to love and respect us. They embraced us as Christian brothers and sisters in Christ. The healing process lingers because we humans have the innate skill of remembering negative behavior along with selective recall about the favorable aspects of events and people.

At this time, an ideal situation developed that afforded me some needed time away from Kitsap County. Agape Unlimited, where I was employed, started a new program called Relapse Prevention. The founder of the program, Terence T. Gorski, a recovering addict, was offering eight weeks of advanced training about Relapse Prevention in Chicago, Illinois. The director of Agape suggested that I attend the training because I was the primary instructor for the Relapse Prevention classes.

I agreed to attend. Cherry and I felt that a few weeks away from each other would be beneficial and give us some time to pray and do some soul-searching about our future. While my children were now grown, our potential marriage would include Cherry's three daughters, two of whom were in high school and the oldest would be beginning her first year in college.

In her divorce settlement, Cherry was given the house, but I felt very uncomfortable over the thought of moving into the home where she and her former husband had lived as a family for about twenty years. The questions swimming around in my mind were probably more about public opinions of my future as well as adjusting to Cherry's daughters and my daughter and son's relationship with my new family. My son, Sam III, did not support the marriage initially, but after some time passed, and we had an honest father-son conversation, things changed. This entire situation was a challenge and I was not mentally and physically prepared for it, and there were some personal adjustments Cherry and I had to make.

Again, those mixed emotions were very real. The question that troubled me was, "Am I ready to enter married life again?" I believed that Cherry and I loved each other, and we had always enjoyed each other's company, yet when the conversations were over, we still both went to our own houses.

My two major concerns at this time boiled down to my entering a second marriage and our church family worshipping in the Masonic Temple rather than a permanent location. The future was cloudy; nevertheless, I recalled the words of a pastor I had known in Colorado: "Show me a person who has never failed, and I will show you a person who has never accomplished very much." The wise person learns from his or her mistakes and moves forward; life evolves forward, not backward. Another old truism I recalled at this time was, "The things we worry about, in most cases, never come to pass."

The few weeks I spent in Chicago were a time of careful, long-range decision making that would have a long-term effect on my life, Cherry's life, and the Mount Zion church family. Ultimately, Cherry and I both decided to enter into marriage.

After I returned from Chicago, the next Sunday after the worship service, I made the announcement of my pending marriage with Cherry. The church members stood up, some shouted, and they began to celebrate with us. What a total and overwhelming surprise this response was to me. The deacons and their wives knew of our intention, but this was the first time I had ever said anything about our relationship to the church body. I was relieved by the membership's approval. Although we had failed God, His grace and mercy shines through and looks past our failures and shows His agape (unconditional) love.

Cherry and I talked with Reverend Brazill about officiating at the marriage ceremony, and he and his wife were very happy to support our decision and blessed our marriage.

I did realize that Reverend Brazill's integrity and credibility would be questioned because of his supporting our marriage, yet he and his wife were willing to take the spiritual risk. Cherry and I have always been eternally grateful to him and Sister Brazill for their loving support.

Cherry and I were married December 28, 1991. The number of people who attended the wedding surprised both Cherry and me. The number of gifts and well wishes we received were beyond our imagination.

During the wedding reception, a few of the church ladies gathered around me and began to talk about relocation. They said, "Pastor, we need to be in a church building to worship and serve God." To the best of my recollection, those ladies included Sister Lisa Thompson, Sister Linda Yerger, and Sister Linda Jones.

I was both somewhat shocked and pleased that they were looking to the future, and I heard forgiveness toward me in their voices; it was like they were saying, "The past is over, so let's move forward because you are our pastor." This conversation reinforced for me the expression "failure is not final." I began to think, "There can be a new beginning for the Mount Zion Baptist Church family."

One of these ladies, Sister Linda Yerger, had invited me to lunch just before I went to my training in Chicago. During lunch, she asked me, "Pastor Rachal, do you intend to remain as the Pastor of Mount Zion?"

I responded, "Yes. I have no plans to leave Bremerton or Mount Zion."

She said, "If you're committed to stay, I am also." To this day, Linda is a loyal and faithful member of Mount Zion.

The meeting with those ladies on my wedding day gave me a spark of spiritual energy and a more positive attitude about the church and my future as pastor. While I did not make any concrete promises that day to the ladies, I did tell them, "I have a chaplain friend, and I will talk with him after the first of the year." With newfound enthusiasm, I believed the membership truly needed a permanent building in which to worship the Lord. Their words of support had ignited my inner spirit and reinforced my faith in God and the love and respect I believed the people of Mount Zion had for me as their pastor, so it now became my passion to find a permanent residence for the Mount Zion family.

One day, I met Chaplain Belcher, the resident chaplain at Harrison Memorial Hospital of Bremerton through the Bremerton Ministerial Alliance. Chaplain Belcher had recruited some of the Alliance members to work weekends as on-call chaplains, which would allow Chaplain Belcher some free weekends to enjoy his family. I had agreed to be one of those on call; the experience was beneficial because it provided me with some training in handling issues such as a sudden death, families dealing with funeral arrangements, and grief counseling.

I called Chaplain Belcher and discussed Mount Zion's situation, including the inconvenience of worshipping in the Masonic Temple, having to use Sinclair Missionary Baptist Church to baptize new converts, and the members wanting to be in a permanent church building.

During our conversation, he said, "Sam, you should talk with Pastor Bill Kittenring. He is the pastor of the Free Methodist Church on Thirteenth Street. I believe he and his congregation wish to relocate to Silverdale. You may be able to use their building."

I thanked him for his advice and hung up the phone. My thoughts were, "A Free Methodist church. Methodist people do not immerse their people during baptism; they just sprinkle water. They probably do not have a baptistery."

A few weeks passed before I took a drive over to the church on Thirteenth Street. The building was an older, white wood-framed building. A tall steeple stood at the top of the entrance, and a few cedar and pine trees stood on the property. The front entrance had a cement walk that led to the door. Beautiful azaleas and a maple tree were a part of the entrance. And there was another entrance from the parking lot.

The parking lot was large, composed of rocks and gravel. A wooden walkway connected it to the church's west side entrance. Also, at the rear of the property was a large, gray framed house, which I assumed was the parsonage.

I walked to the east side of the church building, where there was an entrance to the pastor's office.

When I knocked on the door, Pastor Kittenring answered it. He was a relatively young White man with a receding hair line, chubby, and very friendly. I had met him during an alliance meeting. We greeted one another, and he invited me in. After a few minutes, I said, "Pastor Kittenring, Chaplain Belcher told me that your church family was thinking about moving, and my church is looking for a building to rent."

Pastor Kittenring jumped to his feet and grabbed my hand.

"Yes, we do want to relocate," he said, "and I believe the church family would be very happy about renting you folks the building."

I had never been comfortable with the phrase "you folks." Was it intended as a polite expression or a degrading one? I was even more uncomfortable when a White person used it.

I had a tendency to be uncomfortable in the presence of some Whites because my initial experiences in Kitsap County with select members of the White population had not been very pleasant. Some of the older African Americans who had arrived in Kitsap County from 1945 through the 1960s appeared to be afraid of Caucasians. During my first two years in Kitsap County and as a member of the Bremerton branch of the National Association for the Advancement of Colored People (NAACP), we had conducted a public demonstration of protest against racial biases, such as a cross burning in the yard of an interracial family in Poulsbo and a hanging noose placed over a Black employee's locker at Puget Sound Naval Shipyard (PSNS). During a windstorm once, a tree on the church property on Sylvan Way was about to fall on a neighboring house, and its White owners called a tree service company to cut down the tree and charged the church for the cost. When I filed a claim for reimbursement in small claims court, I couldn't believe the church lost the case, and that one of my parishioners went to the family to apologize for my behavior.

For these reasons, the expression "you folks" was never one of my favorite expressions. Nevertheless, during the conversation with Pastor Kittenring, I tried to set aside such thoughts.

Pastor Kittenring said, "I can set up a meeting with our trustees and discuss the cost and when you folks can occupy the building. How soon can we meet?"

I said, "First, I have to meet with the church, the trustees, and the members to see the building. Should they agree to accept the offer, then we can meet with you folks."

Pastor Kittenring and I talked for a bit, and then we took a walk through the church building. The building had three levels, the main sanctuary, upstairs seating, and a large lower level with a nursery and what could be used as an all-purpose room. My first thought proved true—no baptistery.

Nevertheless, I left the meeting rejoicing. I was happy that Mount Zion could afford the monthly rent, and I prayed that Mount Zion would accept the building. This opportunity truly felt like a God-sent blessing for both Mount Zion and the people of the Free Methodist Church.

During our church business meeting, I told the members about the Free Methodist Church. They asked several questions about the building, but most of them agreed to give it some thought and visit the property. A few weeks later, the church unanimously agreed to rent the building. The meeting between Mount Zion leaders and the Free Methodist group went well, and all the terms of renting the building were defined; everyone agreed to $1,000 per month for rent and a one-year contract.

At that point, Mount Zion's financial picture was still not glamorous. Our monthly payment for the Temple was $500 per month, and we paid $300 rent for storage, which would be eliminated when we moved into the Free Methodist Church. The church body believed another $400-$500 a month in income was possible as our members increased their giving and new members were added to the body. Again, by the grace and mercy of God, our monthly income grew, and the church was able to meet all of its commitments.

Mount Zion was back in a building after about seven years of wandering in the wilderness. However, the Sylvan Way property mortgage payment was still an issue. The church had voted to sell the property on Sylvan Way, yet a primary issue that hindered the sale was that an acre of the land defined by the county as a wetland could not be sold.

This parcel sat at the front of the property, making the land not very attractive to a buyer.

After we moved into the Free Methodist Church, I met with a real estate agent who worked for John L. Scott Real Estate. He was a very personable man who was willing to take on the challenge. Again, with the intervention of God, the realtor found a buyer and sold the land within a year. About the same time the property was sold, the people who owned the Free Methodist Church were interested in selling their property.

We had enough funds after the sale of the property to buy just the church building, but we could not afford the parsonage as well, which would mean dividing up the property. Eventually, the church decided to buy both buildings, and we used a local bank to mortgage the loan with reasonable monthly payments for us.

By the grace and mercy of God, in 1993, Mount Zion Missionary Baptist Church was the owner of a church building and a parsonage—a building we could use for Sunday school, Bible study, and a fellowship hall. Plus the Lord had blessed us with some loving and giving members, and our financial picture was changing.

Soon after the blessing of a new church home came another emotional event; I was presented with the opportunity to serve as vice moderator of the Ebenezer Baptist District Association (EBDA). This organization is composed of ten Baptist churches located in Pierce, Kitsap, and Thurston Counties. The organization's objective was to build spiritual growth and wholesome relationships between the ten churches that made up the organization.

This experience of being selected to serve as moderator of the EBDA was very emotional for me because of how I was harshly rejected by some of my colleagues in the ministry when I first arrived in Kitsap

County, yet it was an excellent learning experience that taught me love, forgiveness, and that wholesome relationships still exist within the Christian family when an individual fails—again, reinforcing the principle, "failure is not final."

In 1990, just before my divorce proceedings started, Reverend Brazill was the moderator of the organization, and I was to be voted in as his vice moderator, which would result in my moving into the position of moderator when Reverend Brazill's three-year tenure was over. The members of the EBDA would vote to accept or reject me as vice moderator. I was going through my divorce at this time, and the news was out about my infidelity. Just before the voting, Reverend Brazill came and sat by me and said, "Do not say anything. You just sit here with me. God has already worked it out."

A year later, I was elected as the moderator for the years 1991-1994. It was an uphill battle because most of the programs I attempted to initiate were voted down or not supported. Yet as Reverend Brazill had stated, "God has already worked it out." There were a few things started under my administration, such as a blanket drive for the homeless, clothing and toys for children whose parents were incarcerated, and an emblem represented by a stone because Ebenezer is a biblical word meaning "stone of help."

In 1997, I was nominated again to serve as moderator, and I am, as of 2012, the only pastor in the EBDA ever to serve two terms.

During this tenure, I had the EBDA bylaws reviewed and updated. I established a yearly budget and policies and procedures to govern the nominating committee. The progress I made as moderator reinforced the spiritual reassurance that failure is not final.

This period in my ministry was a great learning experience for me about people in general. Those people included the families I served as pastor and the families with whom I fellowshipped within the EBDA. In both groups, there were some who were unforgiving initially and some who never showed any change in their attitude toward me or my wife, Cherry. While the fundamental principle of Christianity is that God in Christ forgives sin and all confessed sins are forgiven, yet the remaining consequence of sin is how unforgiving people can be. When we humans fail, we find it very hard to forgive ourselves, and those unforgiving thoughts and feelings are reinforced by our unforgiving neighbors. Our focus must always be on God's grace and mercy that is poured out on the wayward sinner and to remember that with God's help, failure is not final.

By the grace and mercy of God, 1993 began a new season of spiritual growth and development for me as a pastor and for the membership of Mount Zion Missionary Baptist Church of Bremerton. This time showed that both the pastor and the parishioners had some hills to climb, some peaks and valleys to overcome, but in spite of it all, the Lord was placing new members within the church family with a new spirit. There was a new enthusiasm, and I began to see put into practical application those glorious words written by the apostle Peter in the closing chapter of 2 Peter: "But grow in grace and in the knowledge of our Lord Jesus Christ."

After moving into the church building on Thirteenth Street, the church family all agreed that our new surroundings were more pleasant, and we were very happy and began to settle into our new home. Our financial picture was satisfactory, but wisdom said we needed to adjust the design of the building's interior. We were still without a baptistery and a choir stand. Also, my office was adequate, but the space was tight when entertaining visiting pastors and ministers from other churches.

My vision of remodeling the existing building would be a major financial task, and I did not know what kind of financial support I would receive from the congregation. Although Christianity teaches that all things belong to the Lord, people find this concept difficult to grasp, and requesting money is always a very sensitive topic and a difficult hill to climb.

The situation made me recall a proverb from a preacher's sermon: "Much pray, much power; less pray, less power." My petitions and supplications to God were for humility and perseverance.

I wanted this remodeling project to be God's vision for Mount Zion and not a personal ego trip for me as the pastor. A person's personal motivation can be very difficult to separate from God's wishes. The question must always be asked and answered: Am I doing this for vain glory or to glorify God? It is hard to separate human approval from God's approval because human approval is visible, whereas God's approval is not always clear initially, but we must not lose sight that after the task is completed, it is God that receives the glory.

The church's financial secretary, during this period, was very efficient about accounting principles and maintaining accurate financial records. The board of trustees was doing an efficient job in its task to ensure that the building and grounds were in good repair. I must admit, from information I had learned from Reverend Brazill and other pastors, the board of trustees' members had an unwritten law. "The board of trustees is totally independent and personally responsible for all church funds and the disbursement of those funds." The board president submitted a monthly written report to the pastor, informing him of all financial disbursements. Otherwise the policy was hands off regarding how the board of trustees operated, pastor included. Of course, this situation created some unnecessary discussion because in Mount Zion's bylaws, the pastor is ex officio during any church or organization meeting, including the board of trustees. So my strategy was not to speak directly with the board of trustees, but with the deacons. The board of deacons would become my sounding board for how the church members would respond to a remodeling program. I believed that if the board of deacons were supportive of the remodeling program, they could get the trustees' support.

At this time, the board of deacons' members were Chairman Deacon Darrell Monroe, Deacon William Jones, Deacon Michael Gordon, and Deacon Kenneth Riley, who was the youngest member yet a very intelligent young man with leadership potential.

With the board of deacons' blessings, our next hurdle was to gain the church council's support. The council was composed of the church department leaders, such as laymen, the women, youth, music, education, and Sunday school ministries, and members at large. These leaders would have had positive influences within their departments and the membership. My goal was to allow the membership to motivate and ignite a spark in the remodeling program. Experience had taught me that the mind-set of some members was that the church building and all church items belong to the pastor and not the membership. It was my ambition to inform the parishioners that, first, it is the power of the Holy Spirit that governs the church. The pastor has certain leadership power, but the actual voting power, the power to implement major projects, is within the membership. This concept was difficult for some of the older members to accept, because historically, some thought, "What the pastor says is not to be questioned." My objective was to teach the membership that the church employed the pastor, and the voting power was within the church body.

Although some discord existed in the church body, the majority of the members were supportive about the need for a baptistery and a choir section. Some wanted to rebuild within the existing structure and not extend the building. They wrestled with these decisions a bit before we all finally agreed to research the cost for a complete remodeling of the existing structure.

The financial secretary, with the help of the board of trustees, designed a visible graph that described the church income and expenses. The graph also gave a present and future financial picture of how, through personal tithes and sacrificial giving, we could meet the expenses for a remodeling project.

With much discussion, the church voted to establish an ad hoc remodeling committee. This committee was tasked with securing three bids from an architect to design plans for remodeling the church, which included a baptistery, choir stand, pastor's office, secretary's office, and installing the stained glass windows from the previous building. The baptistery would change the structure and size of the pulpit, pastor's office, and carpet for the sanctuary.

After a few glitches, we finally secured an architect, and after designing the plans for the remodeling and necessary landscaping work, the committee secured three bids from local construction companies.

I sincerely believe God gave His ordained blessing about the excavation around the building. I was determined that an excavation was necessary to secure the foundation that would extend the existing building's rear. The son of a woman within the church, who was a heavy equipment operator, did all of the excavation necessary for the foundation at no cost to the church. This contribution was a huge financial savings for the church and a God-sent blessing.

We continued to worship in the building while most of the outside and downstairs work was done. The contractors informed the committee that we would need to vacate the building for about a month. During that time, Sinclair Missionary Baptist, our sister church, was gracious enough to allow us to worship with its congregation during Sunday worship and Wednesday night Bible study. This type of blessing benefited both congregations by helping us to develop a lasting relationship between the two church families.

In June 2002, we relocated back to our newly remodeled building, delighted that God had provided a permanent home for Mount Zion. This homecoming was an exciting and joyful time for the Mount Zion family, and we rejoiced in the Lord. I was grateful and thankful to our Lord and savior for His grace and mercy and the guidance of the Holy Spirit. There is no doubt in my mind and heart that humility coupled with agape love were the unseen ingredients that united the church's efforts to bring about this success. God had delivered this loyal group of people from many years in the wilderness back to an edifice blessed by God for His people to worship and to serve their living savior.

For me, this homecoming was my greatest accomplishment as a leader, in conjunction with acceptance of my divine call to the ministry. The storms of life were not over, but just for the moment, I could see bright sunshine. This huge burden of guilt and failure was lifted from my heart.

After moving into our new building, the church family settled in to worshiping God and reorganizing the church education program. We developed a Christian Education Board, whose task was to educate our people. The church membership consisted of some very loyal and dedicated members, yet a large portion of them did not understand how a church operated. Our people worked and lived in the secular world, which was very different from how we operate in the spiritual world. All tasks are done through the efforts of volunteers and require dedication, loyalty, and a steadfast commitment. The tasks require talents and time, and the rewards are precious, but they are not of material, but spiritual value.

Christians must clearly understand that God wants the person first, then their time and talents, and then financial resources—tithes and offerings. Every Christian should be filled with the Holy Spirit, wisdom, and have a good report within the secular community as these requirements are essential for leaders.

The church family made a unanimous agreement that all leaders must attend leadership training to help identify their spiritual gifts. This training was conducted once a month, and it was available for all members. Job descriptions were developed for all leaders, such as moderator, minister of music, trustee chairperson, etc. This training program was a giant step in our church family's growth and development. As new people joined the church family, they were trained by department leaders.

Our Christian Education Board also initiated a Spirit Awards program. This yearly event was held in October; it recognized, by secret ballot, members of the church family who projected growth and dedication in categories such as efficiency as a leader, support of church activities and worship service, Sunday school, and Bible study, and dedicated teachers in our Sunday school and Junior Church. The Spirit Awards program became a vital part of our church because it afforded our members a reason to dress-up—ladies wore long dresses and men wore tuxedoes.

One of our members was a young lady who possessed the talents to be a stand-up comedian. She developed a character, Ms. Cora, who had a boyfriend named Big John. Ms. Cora was a large woman with a large bust and rear. Her dress was colorful; she always carried a big leather bag and loved to talk on her cell phone. Her favorite pastimes were playing bingo and the lottery. She promised the pastor that should she win enough money, she would pay her tithes to help build a new building. She loved to gossip and had trouble pronouncing my and Cherry's names. She called us Pastor Rascal and Sister Strawberry. Ms. Cora became the center of entertainment for most of Mount Zion's fellowship celebrations.

The twenty-one plus years I served as pastor of the Mount Zion Missionary Baptist Church in Bremerton were filled with times of delightful joy and events that rocked the core of my human emotions.

Jonathan Edwards, the eighteenth century Puritan preacher who delivered the classic sermon, "Sinners in the Hands of an Angry God," stated that everything we humans are or can be is of God. God's grace and mercy give us salvation through the death of His son, Jesus the Christ; God gave us His word, the Bible. Edwards wrote, "'The ministers of God and all their sufficiency are of Him.' (2 Corinthians 6:7) We have this treasure in earthen vessels that the Excellency of the power may be of God and not of us. Our success as ministers of the Gospel depends entirely and absolutely on the immediate blessing and influence of God."

When I first read these words of Edwards and what Paul wrote in 2 Corinthians 6:7 and I internalized its meaning, my daily anxious moments of despair were lifted. I began to realize that I was employed by a sovereign God who was active in my life and in my ministry as a pastor. I had to do my part, such as read, study, meditate, pray, and seek spiritual wisdom from spiritual people and remember that I was never alone in my ministry. As one wise person wrote, "Do all that you can do and leave the rest to God."

In 2004, during my monthly meeting with the board of deacons, I expressed my desire to retire as pastor of Mount Zion. My plans were to serve one more year and take the time and foresight to prepare the people for my retirement. Five ministers were serving at Mount Zion at this time: one elder minister, a wife and husband who were both ministers, and two middle-aged men. These ministers were not ordained, which is a requirement for a Baptist pastor. Some pastors select a person to be the next pastor, but I did not want to make that decision. I felt that if I should recommend someone and he or she was not successful, I would be accused of recommending the wrong person. But if the church made the selection, then I would be accused of not telling the congregation whom to select. It was a no-win situation for me as the outgoing pastor.

Before my retirement, I did ordain the wife and husband team, Ministers Mack and Rose Litton, to serve as interim pastors until the church selected a permanent pastor. After my retirement, this husband-and-wife team felt it unfair that I did not allow them to be candidates, although I had explained to them that it was the policy of most Baptist churches that the interim pastor(s) could not submit their names as candidates for the pastor. The Pastoral Search Committee allowed them to enter the process, but they were not selected. They removed their membership from Mount Zion and started their own church, and they are now doing excellent work for the Lord.

As the Bible tells us, God's ways are neither our ways, nor God's thoughts like our thoughts; we look at the outer appearance, but God knows the heart (Isaiah 55:8; 1 Samuel 16:7). I believed the Littons were sincere about serving God yet not ready to pastor a church. But who can know the mind of God? It was another magnificent learning experience for me about how God uses people.

Looking back now, I can truly say that from the beginning of my ministry as pastor of the Mount Zion Missionary Baptist Church, my thoughts and aspirations were to "Do what is best for the church body, never what is best for me or my family." This concept was always my prayer, and with much soul-searching over this situation, I asked this one question, "What was best for the people of Mount Zion?"

When you know in your heart, in your inner person, that your desire and aspiration is first to glorify God and that your primary ambition is to help improve people's spiritual lives through biblical teaching to enhance their growth and development, it can be difficult when your actions are received with skepticism and backbiting. The most excruciating pain is rejection. It is an unseen scar that is very slow to heal.

As with any career, being a pastor has its dark days and some enjoyable days. During my career as a pastor, my time was composed of both, yet to be very honest, most of my experiences were beneficial, and my call to the ministry was the greatest act of God in my life. My yielding to the Divine guidance of His Holy Spirit is the greatest decision I have ever made. All praise to God and the person who said these words to me many years ago: "Show to me a person who has never failed, and I will show to you a person who has not accomplished very much" because "failure is not final."

With unwavering faith in God and the resilience to recover and learn invaluable lessons from all of life's experiences in my developing years, my military years, and as the church pastor of God's people, I have known the most rich and rewarding experiences of my life to this point.

God only knows what my future shall be, yet I know who holds the future, and I know who holds my hands. Daily, I live with the "Blessed Assurance" that I am a child of the King, and Jesus truly changed my whole life.

Edwin Tegenfeldt

Remembrances and Thoughts about Mount Zion Missionary Baptist Church: 1992-2004

Edwin and Margaret Tegenfeldt were members of Mount Zion during much of the time I was pastor there. I thought it would be interesting to my readers to read the viewpoints of these two active members of the church during that time, so I am sharing their reflections here with their permission.

Sister Margaret and I joined Mount Zion in January of 1992, when the church was meeting in the rented Masonic Lodge on Burwell Street.

We had returned from twenty years of medical mission service in India in June of 1991. At a missionary conference in August of 1991, we were privileged to have one of the speakers be an African American pastor from a church in New York. As we had an adopted African American daughter, we spoke with this pastor about our thoughts of joining an African American church to expose her to traditions and forms of worship from her heritage that she had missed out on while growing up in India. He not only thought that would be a good idea, but he encouraged us also from the standpoint of missions because he said most

African American churches in the USA were not involved in mission outreach and participating in the great commission of Christ. As former missionaries under the American Baptist Church, we were interested in continuing those ties and hence looked for an African American church in Kitsap County that was aligned with the American Baptist Church. As there were two such churches, we visited both Sinclair and Mount Zion. We were attracted to Mount Zion, so we began attending there and finally joined in early 1992.

Early impressions included different traditions and worship styles that we had not been used to, but we enjoyed more participatory congregation worship both in the music as well as during the sermons. We were used to being of a minority race in our experiences in the Indian churches, and so we felt we were very much a part of the church family, and race never played a part during all of our experiences there. We also enjoyed the Bible teaching and preaching of Pastor Rachal.

As we became more involved and attended business meetings, we saw that the church operated more on traditions, and there were areas of church governance which could stand some improvement. As in other churches where we had been members, there were points of friction between the pastor and some of the members, but it appeared that some of these could be overcome by developing a better church constitution. This was especially true in matters between the trustee board and the pastor. However, it was apparent that several of the church members were opposed to the pastor for other reasons, and this came to the forefront at business meetings and even developed to the point where a vote was scheduled for the church to decide whether to keep or dismiss the pastor. Pastor Rachal handled this very difficult situation with humility and faith, and by the grace of God, the church voted to retain him. I had had some experience with budgets in the mission work in India, so I agreed when I was asked to develop a budget process for the church. It required a bit of an educational process for the church, both in developing a budget as well as being governed by a budget. Later, I was happy to see the church go into a very inclusive process of developing a church constitution and adopting that.

Some of the changes we have seen at Mount Zion under the pastoral leadership of Rev. Rachal are the following:

1. A teaching ministry helping new members grow and mature in discipleship.
2. Purchasing a church building.
3. The church began looking outward and getting involved with outreach mission.
4. Mentoring young ministers.

It has been a great blessing for me to be an integral part of the Mount Zion church family.

Margaret Tegenfeldt

Reflections on Our Time at Mount Zion

The first time we came to Mount Zion was toward the end of 1991, when it was on Burwell, and we had a hard time finding the church. We found an address in the yellow pages, but there was no Mount Zion to be seen at that site. A phone call directed us to downtown Bremerton, and we eventually found our way up to the second floor hall in the Masonic Lodge, where the worship services were being held. Of course, the ushers were very welcoming, and so were many others during the fellowship time in the midst of the service. Pastor Rachal wanted to know whether Ed was a pastor, and if so, wanted to invite him to sit up on the podium. We explained that we had just moved to Washington after twenty years as missionaries in India, but we were not pastors and were happy to sit in the congregation. After attending for a number of weeks, we both felt that Mount Zion was God's choice of a church home for us in Kitsap County. I'm sure many in the Mount Zion family may have wondered why we joined that church, but they opened their arms to us in ways we found quite amazing, especially since so many had experienced discrimination at the hands of White people.

Brother Ed and I looked different from most of the other members, and we thought differently in a number of ways, but that was accepted, and we could be comfortable in being who we were, at least most of the time. That was reassuring because sometimes, in White congregations, we looked the same as everyone else, but we still thought differently because of our years in other countries both as children and as adults. Some people could not understand that and kept expecting us to be more American. Of course, it took us a little while to get into the right rhythm with clapping our hands and moving our feet and bodies to the music, but I really enjoyed the music and participating with my body as well as with my voice. Brother Ed found doing that a bit of a challenge when he was in the choir and also trying to remember the words and sing a bass part with no sheet of music to follow! But he enjoyed being a part of the choir until his work schedule made it impossible for him to get to choir practice.

We had been exposed to many styles of worship because of the ecumenical and international worship services we were used to, so we were happy to learn the African American way of worship as well. However, whenever it seemed to be implied that the Holy Spirit was at work only when the congregation was involved in standing or waving arms or saying amen, I felt perhaps that my sitting quietly might be misjudged. The Holy Spirit has often worked in my life during times of quiet reflection and meditation on God's Word, whether in reading it or in hearing it preached. I also felt that the impact of the Holy Spirit's presence in the church should be measured more by the fruits of the spirit lived out in the lives of the members in the world than by what was said or done during a worship service. That does not mean that the ways in which others responded were not meaningful and important for them in their response to the spirit, but just that I did not want to be expected to respond in the same way. That being said, I very much enjoyed the experience of worship at Mount Zion.

It was more difficult for me to get used to the pattern used for Sunday school classes. We were asked to read our upcoming lesson at home, but then most of the class time was used to take turns reading sections aloud in the class time. I eventually realized that this was probably a tradition started years and years ago, when many of the members were illiterate and still being carried on without question for the sake of tradition. There also did not seem to be any thought of offering different ideas than those presented in the study book but just accepting it all as the true interpretation. Anyway, when I was asked to teach a class, I resorted to the way I was used to and tried to lead a discussion of various interpretations of the Scripture lesson and how it might apply to our lives today. So when the Sunday school superintendent resigned and I was asked to take over for the rest of his term, I reluctantly agreed, and I tried to introduce these changes more widely. But I had not been there long enough, and I didn't understand well enough what was comfortable and useful for the members. It was not a good fit for me in that position, and it was not helpful for Mount Zion, although there were a few who attended some of the classes I taught who seemed to appreciate my style of teaching with increased class participation.

Soon after we joined Mount Zion, I wanted to participate in what I thought was a missions program, and so I started attending the Ladies' Mission meetings. However, I could not find anything resembling the mission's emphasis of the Women's Missionary societies in the American Baptist churches with which I was familiar. The focus seemed to be on planning fellowship meetings with the women of other churches and sometimes on raising money for scholarships for young people within the Ebenezer Association. These were worthwhile endeavors but not what I thought of as missions. When I told Pastor Rachal that I did not want to continue as Sunday school superintendent, I also said that

I would like to try to do something else, and that was to try to educate the congregation about what "mission" meant to me and why I thought it was important for the church. I told him that mission for me meant reaching out with evangelism and practical help to those *outside* the church. I am very, very grateful for his encouragement and support for something totally new to the life of Mount Zion. We called the new program Outreach Ministry, so as not to confuse it with the women's "mission" program. Through Outreach Moments during the worship service once a month, I tried to help the congregation become aware of outreach activities in the United States and around the world and encouraged them to think and pray about how they, as individuals and as a church, could become involved in Outreach. That first year, Pastor and I met together to choose some projects which could be supported with specific offerings which members of the congregation chose to give. The next year, I told Pastor that if the Outreach Ministry were going to be sustained, it could not be seen as *my* ministry but would need to be owned and run by the church. So I asked whether I could ask for volunteers for an outreach committee, and he agreed. I was so pleased that several responded to my invitation and were willing to work with me. We had monthly meetings in which we suggested new projects, prayed about them, and discussed how to promote the ones we decided to support. The next step was that Outreach Ministry was included by the council in the annual budget of the church, so it was no longer dependent only on specific offering gifts, although that opportunity remained as well. Being in the general budget helped it to become a part of the work of the whole church. Gradually, various members became active in Habitat for Humanity, the Lord's Diner, Crop Walk, and other local programs, and we also continued financially to support a number of ministries around the world. An important boost to the outreach program was the visit of Charles West, an American Baptist missionary in South Africa (now in Zambia). But the highlight of my experience with outreach at Mount Zion was taking a team to Mexico with Brother Ed's help as coleader.

We went for a week to help build a large dining/meeting hall for a Christian camp and to work and worship and fellowship with Mexican Baptists while we were there. It was also an important exposure to another country for many team members. We held preparatory meetings for the team in advance and had a workday at the church to help develop teamwork and to thank the church for donations toward the expenses of the trip. After we returned, we had a program of slides and reports about the trip to share it with the Mount Zion family. Another great source of satisfaction for me has been having a Mount Zion outreach committee member choose to spend a year and a half as a volunteer in mission outreach work in Thailand and Liberia.

Although Outreach Ministry was somewhat new to

Pastor Rachal, when it started, he already had a heart of concern for the needs of people outside of, as well as within, the church. I appreciated his vision to use the parsonage, which the church bought when it bought the church property, to provide housing for some poor family or families, along with providing the church with a fellowship hall. That decision about buying the parsonage and how it would be used created some controversies in the following years, but I am happy to know that it is being used today in the One Church One Family program to help a family in need of a home.

I personally felt very grateful to Pastor Rachal for support and encouragement when I was feeling called by God in new directions and definitely feeling spiritually stretched to follow those calls. He gave me advice and support in joining in a prison ministry, which was something totally new for me. And then he also offered support, although perhaps not agreement with my decision, when I felt called to go to Iraq with the Christian Peacemaker Teams just before the U.S. invasion. I was grateful for his prayers and for those of the church and also for being given a forum to talk about my experiences when I returned. My action in going violated U.S. laws, and he could have been criticized for giving me that opportunity to speak about it in a church meeting.

Brother Ed and I have been very thankful for a growing friendship with Pastor Sam and Sister Cherry as we grew to understand each other better and to respect our occasional differing perspectives. We knew we shared a commitment to learning and growing as followers of Jesus and to helping the church learn and grow as well. I praise God for my time at Mount Zion and the impact of Pastor Rachal and all of the church family on my life. I am thankful for the opportunity God gave me to be a part of the Outreach Ministry and for seeing the way it has continued to grow and flourish even after we moved away from Kitsap County. Mount Zion and the Rachals will always be our family!

Papa's El Camino

The thought behind the painting Papa's El Camino was to reflect the relationship that many men have with their rides . . . for Papa it was the El Camino. It came to my understanding that years ago Papa had given his car away or sold it. With that in mind, my wife thought it would be great to gift him a painting for his 75th birthday so he could remember the fond relationship he once had, but with a few extra symbolic helpings of love.
—Hasaan Kirkland (son-in-law)

Chapter One: A Leap of Faith: "When you know about God's amazing grace, you will show more of God's grace—sometimes it takes a leap of faith."—Pastor Sam Rachal, Jr.

The scene of the composition is positioned just overlooking a body of water accompanied by green foliage to reflect Papa's many travels through the military and his overseas experience as well as his close relationship to the country and water near Shreveport, Louisiana as a young man. This symbolic imagery characterizes what it takes to take a leap of faith to walk out of the conditions that raise a man to a new place that will train a man to a place that will then require him to learn, live, and grow by faith. This imagery illustrates the nature of faith and what it takes truly to walk on water by keeping one's eyes on Christ when taking life-changing leaps of faith into the life God has destined for you.

Chapter Two: The Honeymoon: "A church family is the bride of the pastor; first, there's the honeymoon; then true love, plus conflict, ensues."—Pastor Sam Rachal, Jr.

The old porch and shed symbolize another of his favorite things, a garage or tool shed. This place for Papa is a place that he enjoys much like a private church where he can do many things from praying and talking with the Lord to fixing machines as in his body, intelligence, and mind-set, gardening as in relationships and careers or simply having a quiet place to be as in being in prayer, meditation, or cultivating vision and dreams. All of these experiences are tailored with favor, trepidation, conflicts, and comforts.

Chapter Three: The Tragedy: "The greatest tragedy is not failing, but giving up and not trying again—rest a while, but never quit."—Pastor Sam Rachal, Jr.

In the corner of the composition sits a potted plant with the name Bear painted around the top of it. The name Bear is a nickname for his lovely wife, Cherry Ann. Inside the pot are two types of flowers: one, a white calla lily, and the other, a red rose. The calla lily reflects Papa himself and his two beautiful biological children, Jarutha and Frankie, and the red rose reflects his wife, Cherry Ann, and her beautiful children Stacie, Tiffany, and Amber. This symbol portrays a life again. The pain of a broken family without question breaks the heart and spirit of many men, but the healing power of God mends and restores the heart, mind, love, vision, and will for any man never to give up on what God puts in him to cultivate and harvest. Papa's second family (wife, daughters, sons, and grandchildren) epitomizes his willingness not to quit or to give up on the promises of God.

Chapter Four: The Road Back from Failure: "It is very difficult to be humble if you are always successful, so God chastises us with failure at times in order to humble us, to keep us in a state of humility."—D. Martyn Lloyd-Jones (1899-1981)

The elongated El Camino has been expressionistically fashioned to symbolize the span of Papa's long and blessed life. This life symbolizes his strengths and weaknesses, his moments of glory, and his moments of pain. In every man's life, there are pivotal moments that galvanize his ability to stand up strong and personify his character and his soul. His ability to live through his failures and his triumphs have been reflected in the regal presence of his royal deep wine-colored El Camino, the car that carries the man on the long road of his life.

Chapter Five: Failure is Not Final: "It's okay to fail, but do not quit; the resilient spirit rises up from a failure."—Pastor Sam Rachal, Jr.

There are three crosses in the composition compassed around the car, symbolizing the Father, Son, and the Holy Ghost. The first cross, created by a tire jack, is found leaning up against the rear wheel, casting a long shadow that stretches underneath the vehicle symbolizing the Holy Ghost/God's presence in the foundation of Papa's life. The tire jack symbolizes moments of breakdown and the need for repair. Repair in life and in spirit is something coached and managed by the support of the Holy Spirit. The second cross is found on the roof of the shed, symbolizing Christ/God's presence, an example of being the head of the house and the shelter of his life. This cross above the shed reflects the leadership and the Spirit of God as the head of the home and the church, a position that requires resilient patience, purposeful focus, and prayerful vision. A spirit cultivated by mirroring the Father above. Lastly, a cross created by the telephone pole positioned at the front of the composition near the front of the El Camino symbolizes God's heavenly and earthly presence lifted high in the air. At anytime and anywhere, Papa has access to the Father by his constant prayer and relationship—one that is only a word away. This last symbolic cross exudes the constant availability and access one has in the midst of life when failure or success occurs. God's presence is the recognition of faith if one truly believes. When you do believe, you constantly allow the journey of faith to create the presence of mind for one to live, knowing that your failings are never final.

Edwards Brothers Malloy
Thorofare, NJ USA
August 12, 2013